PRAISE FOR AFTER ZERO

"A powerful and poetic novel about the power of words to shape who we are and who we can be. Elise's journey will speak to anyone who has struggled to find their voice, overcome their doubts, and discover their own self-worth."

—John David Anderson, author of *Posted* and *Ms. Bixby's Last Day*

"*After Zero* takes us into the world of selective mutism and helps us find a story in the silence. For an interconnected generation that can sometimes assume silence is ignorance or a personal slight, this is a must-read. Readers will take to Elise right away: she is smart and earnest, and like many of us, social norms can elude her. The story moves along quickly to broach themes of forgiveness and friendship. But most importantly, it reminds us of so many loved ones of those suffering from anxiety or depressive disorders who want to shout, 'Just speak! Just say something! Just be normal!' Now we get to walk with Elise and understand her struggles. It is a story that will hopefully foster empathy and maybe even communication with all our 'quiet' peers."

—Wesley King, author of *OCDaniel*

"A gripping debut novel about a girl struggling to find her voice and discover her past."

—Carol Weston, author of *Speed of Life* and *Girltalk*

"An eloquent journey through the pain of growing up, this tender and truthful book stays with you long after the words have gone."

—Patricia Forde, author of *The List*

"Collins offers readers a compassionate portrait of selective mutism. Elise is so sensitively drawn, a truly memorable character."

—Sally J. Pla, author of *The Someday Birds* and *Stanley Will Probably Be Fine*

after

ZERO

after

ZERO

CHRISTINA COLLINS

Published by Sourcebooks Jabberwocky, an imprint of Sourcebooks, Inc.
P.O. Box 4410, Naperville, Illinois 60567-4410
(630) 961-3900
Fax: (630) 961-2168
sourcebooks.com

Library of Congress Cataloging-in-Publication Data

Names: Collins, Christina, author.
Title: After zero / Christina Collins.
Description: Naperville, Illinois : Sourcebooks Jabberwocky, [2018] | Summary: When Elise leaves homeschooling for public school, she copes by speaking as little as possible, but soon her silence becomes an impediment to friendship and to dealing with family secrets.
Identifiers: LCCN 2017045912 | (13 : alk. paper)
Subjects: | CYAC: Selective mutism--Fiction. | Interpersonal relations--Fiction. | Schools--Fiction. | Secrets--Fiction. | Ravens--Fiction.
Classification: LCC PZ7.1.C64474 Aft 2018 | DDC [Fic]--dc23 LC record available at https://lccn.loc.gov/2017045912

Source of Production: LSC Communications, Harrisonburg, Virginia, United States
Date of Production: July 2018
Run Number: 5012659

Printed and bound in the United States of America.
LSC 10 9 8 7 6 5 4 3 2 1

For mute swans, lone ravens,
and "other birds" around the world

AND NOW AS SHE DARED TO OPEN HER
MOUTH AND SPEAK...

—Jacob and Wilhelm Grimm (translator
Margaret Hunt), "The Twelve Brothers"

CHAPTER 1

I T'S AMAZING HOW FEW words a person can get by with.

I scratch a tally mark into my notebook and grin. Yesterday it was two, and three the day before that. Today it's one. One word all morning: a new record. If Mr. Scroggins hadn't asked me to name the capital of Russia last period, it could have been zero.

When Miss Looping turns from the board, I move my pencil so it looks like I'm taking notes. I almost feel sorry about not paying attention—Miss Looping isn't so bad. She wears dark velvet dresses and is in love with Charles Dickens. Her stuffed raven, Beady, keeps looking at me. I sneak glances at his perch, waiting for him to open his beak and *kraaa*. But he never moves.

Maybe it's Beady's stare or Miss Looping's dresses or her pasty skin that makes people wonder about her. Most students think she's weird. I don't mind her. She doesn't call on me or hold class discussions. Mr. Gankle and Ms. Dively like that sort of thing, so they never give me A's. Neither does Mrs. Bebeau, who thinks the best way to learn French is to speak it aloud. Miss Looping is the only one who doesn't penalize me for not talking. She puts A's on all my papers and jots comments in the margins—things like "good point" and "nice word choice"—and recommends poets I might like. Sometimes I add a note back to her: Thanks for understanding, Miss L. But she never gets the note because you don't give papers back to teachers after they're graded.

"*Aaaa-choo!*"

I jump as Arty Pilger sneezes next to me, spraying my arm.

I hate when people sneeze. Not because of the spraying—well, that too—but because they expect me to say "bless you." Or "God bless you" if they believe in God.

Someone across the room yells "*Gesundheit,*" and I relax. My tally remains one.

But lunch is next, and that will be trickier. People like to talk at lunch. I look back at the tally mark in my notebook. If I want my record to last more than three periods, I need a new tactic for the cafeteria today. A stronger shield, harder armor.

When the bell rings, I hurry past Beady, avoiding his gaze. I wish Miss Looping would turn him to face the wall. In the hallway, I empty my books into my locker, all except for one this time. Then I make my way to the cafeteria, armed and ready.

I slip into my seat at the end of Mel's table. Mel, Sylvia, Nellie, and Theresa are deep in conversation and don't pause at my arrival. They never do these days. Sometimes their eyes slide sideways, but I don't always see this because I keep my own eyes down.

I pull *The Oxford Book of Sonnets* out of my bag, open it, and eat my sandwich. I get through a whole poem without anyone trying to talk to me. Two poems. Two and a half. Why didn't I think of this before? Read a book—such a simple solution.

"You're reading at lunch?"

Sylvia's voice clangs against my armor. I keep my eyes on the page.

"It must be a good book then."

I force my eyes to move left to right, left to right. If I don't, they'll think I heard. They'll think I'm faking. I can feel them all looking. To these girls, I'm the elephant in the room. And no one can really relax when there's an elephant in the room, least of all the elephant. I've tried sitting at an empty table, but that makes everyone stare more. Like it or not, sitting at Mel's table is better than sitting alone.

"I'm so jealous of your eyebrows." Sylvia's voice again. "I swear they get bigger every day."

No one responds, so I know her words are meant for me. I try to focus on the typeface in front of me. It blurs. I drag my eyes away in spite of myself and find Sylvia in the seat next to Mel, slowly twirling a french fry between her fingers, a smirk playing on the corner of her lip.

Mel shifts in her seat. "I think they're pretty." She must still feel an obligation toward me, considering she's my neighbor and all—and the closest thing I have to a friend. She's too late, though. I'm already scanning the other girls' eyebrows, noting the safe, sure spaces between them—and fighting the urge to reach up and feel mine.

Sylvia's french fry pauses at Mel's comment, but only for a split second. Her smirk doesn't budge. "I could have fixed them for you at Nellie's sleepover Saturday. Why didn't you come?"

An open-ended question—Sylvia's specialty. She sits back and takes a bite of her fry, waiting, watching me. Everyone watches me. Everyone except Mel, who's examining her food.

I push my tongue against my teeth. One word, any word, and I can start over. I can wipe the slate clean, and they'll forget I haven't spoken at this table in the past ten minutes.

Or the past week.

Or the past seven months.

Sweat collects under my arms. I can feel it happening—my throat closing up. The bubble forming. The cop-out coming. Here it comes: My shoulders move up and down in a quick motion. A shrug.

Sylvia cocks her head. "You're awfully quiet today."

Today. As if it's different from any other day.

"Give her a break." Mel picks up her soda and stirs the straw. The ice crashes together.

Sylvia's smirk flickers. She shoots Mel a look. "Why? Didn't her parents teach her how to talk?"

"She talks."

"When?"

Mel concentrates on her food. I try to catch her eye, but I'm losing her. The longer I go without saying something, the more tired she grows of defending me. One of these days, she might stop altogether.

Hours pass, or maybe seconds, before someone changes the subject to something about the sleepover last Saturday. They always lose interest in the elephant eventually. I can count on that.

I return to the page where I left off.

But my eyes slide upward. Faces look at me funny—funnier than usual. No one else in the cafeteria is reading. The point of the book was to draw attention away from me, to show that I'm busy, unavailable, otherwise engaged. But it's backfiring. I close the book, pick up my bag, and leave the cafeteria. Mel doesn't call after me.

I go back to Miss Looping's room, still empty except for Beady. I'll have to put up with him staring. At least he won't talk to me. And if Miss Looping comes back early, she won't try to make small talk like the other teachers. She'll let me be.

I sit in the back row near the open window and return to my book. Something moves in the corner of my eye. I look over to Miss Looping's desk, where Beady is watching me. A fly buzzes past. I swat at it and try to keep reading, but the print blurs worse than before. Instead of poetry, I see Sylvia's smirk all over the page.

You're awfully quiet today. You're awfully quiet today.

My teeth grind. I slam the book shut and punch it with the side of my fist. At the same time, a black shape leaps in my periphery and another noise shakes the room—a shattering of ceramic. I jerk my head up to find Beady on the floor near Miss Looping's desk, rocking on his side. Miss Looping's "What the Dickens!" coffee mug lies in pieces next to him.

I grab my book and bolt out the door, my heart thudding.

Relax, I tell myself as I stumble down the hall. He's a stuffed bird. Top-heavy, that's all. Top-heavy things tip over sometimes.

Still, there's something about Beady I've never trusted. His feathers are too feather-like, his talons too talon-like. I walk faster, turning left and right under the glare of fluorescent lights, down more halls with burnt-orange walls. Farther ahead now I see double doors and a sign. A word in block letters:

QUIET

I slow, squinting. The word follows me. Haunts me. It won't leave me alone. I can't remember when people started using it—there must have been a day, a moment—but it's all I've heard since then.

Elise is so quiet.

Elise, you've been quiet. What do you think about such and such?

That's her over there. The quiet one.

Mr. Scroggins writes the same note on all my social studies papers: *Terrific work, Elise. You present a strong, fluid argument. But I wish you'd speak up more in class. You're very quiet.*

I try to ignore the word, but there's something about it. Something that tells me it isn't a compliment.

QUIET

Now it appears as illusions on the walls. What next? Voices in my head? Tightening my fists, I walk toward the sign. I'll break the illusion. I'll stare it down and scare it away.

The rest of the sign comes into focus.

QUIET

IN THE LIBRARY

The words wink at me. I blink and read them again.

The librarian doesn't notice me come in. Her back is turned as she arranges books on a shelf. Bernard Billows snoozes at a table in the corner, wearing the same T-shirt and sweatpants he wears every day. I can smell his spoiled-milk cologne from here. No one else is in the library. It must not be a popular lunch spot. I've been here only once, seven months ago after the second day of school, back when I was still curious about everything. I'd never seen a public-school library before. But I left after two minutes—there were too many people here then, the jigsaw puzzle club or something.

Green Pasture Middle School loves that club stuff. They have this initiative where every student has to join at least one club or team before spring vacation. The principal keeps reminding us in his intercom announcements. Mel and Sylvia and all of them are in the choir and the drama club. I still haven't joined anything.

I sit at a table in the farthest corner of the library, near the poetry section, and open my book. It takes me a minute to find my place. Before long, I actually turn a page. And another. No eyes stare at me this time. No one tries to talk to me. I decide to come back for lunch the next day. And maybe even the next.

A bird croaks outside the window, but I refuse to let it break my concentration.

I can already taste the victory of tomorrow's tally: zero.

CHAPTER 2

M Y MOTHER CATCHES ME as I sneak past the kitchen. "How was school?"

"Good," I say. She has no reason to believe this isn't true. She never gets calls of concern from Green Pasture. Why would she? I'm passing my classes, and the teachers are all too busy keeping the loud kids quiet to worry about the quiet kid. So I keep feeding her the same answer, and she keeps gobbling it up. And it never affects my tally because there's no counting at home. There's no need for it. We hardly talk to each other as it is, and when we do, there's nothing to lose. She'll still be my mother no matter what comes out of my mouth.

"What do you think?" She holds up the hat she's knitting at the kitchen table. "Got an order on my website today."

"It's nice." I never criticize her handiwork. Just like I never ask why she doesn't have a real job in an office building, like Mel's parents. For as long as I can remember, she's been working from home, selling—or trying to sell—her knitwear, and teaching online college math. And, up until seven months ago, homeschooling me, if that counts as a job—though she never showed any enthusiasm for it.

She returns to her work now, and I continue on my way.

I stop in the bathroom and lean close to the mirror. Fine hairs cascade from my eyebrows, reaching toward the area above my nose. Almost touching. Almost an *M*.

I open the cabinet and fumble through my mother's things: powder, lotion, nail clippers, tweezers. I take out the tweezers, grip a hair, and pull. Nothing happens. I yank harder. A twinge rips through my skin. I shut my eyes. I open them, and my vision is watery. One hair down. It will take forever this way. There must be a quicker method.

I pull back the shower curtain and eye my mother's razor. I never use her things—she doesn't like me touching them—but this is an emergency. I wet the razor in the sink and hold it between my eyebrows, sliding it sideways.

I lower the razor. In the mirror, one eyebrow is shorter than the other. Way shorter. My palms sweat. I have to make them even. I can't go to school like this. I rinse the razor and lift it again.

"What are you... Don't *do* that."

I see my mother in the mirror staring at me. I should

have locked the door. She has a quiet way of entering rooms sometimes.

She comes forward and rips the razor from my hand. "Why'd you do that?"

"A girl at school said I have a unibrow."

"That's ridiculous. You don't have a unibrow."

"That's because I just shaved it."

"You shouldn't do that. It'll grow back thicker and all stubbly."

"It's not fair. Your eyebrows are fine."

"Your father had the Armenian genes. Blame him."

"Did he have a unibrow too?"

"You don't have a unibrow."

"I bet he wouldn't lie to me."

My mother's eyes flash. I've seen it before: that glint of loathing. Whether the loathing is for me or my father, or both, I'm not sure. "You think your father never lied? If you'd known him…"

I wait, holding my breath. She never talks about him.

She sets down the razor and grabs an eye pencil from the cabinet. "Here…use this to fill in the shorter one till it grows back. Now can I use the bathroom?"

I stare at the eye pencil. She's never given me anything

of her own before. My stubbornness tells me not to trust it, to refuse this gesture of pity or charity or whatever it is. But in the mirror I see the unevenness again. It does look pretty bad.

"Fine." I grab the pencil and march past her to my room.

I don't bother slamming the door. I plop onto my bed and put the eye pencil on my dresser. It's the only makeup item in my room. I wonder if Mel owns makeup. I've never seen her wear any. Sylvia does. Powdery stuff always cakes her pimples, and clumps of mascara cling to her eyelashes. Would it make a difference if I wore any? Can makeup make up for other things, like being "quiet"?

I listen to my mother's footfalls as I do my homework. *Creak, creak, creak* to the kitchen. *Creak, creak, creak* to her bedroom. For someone so good at sneaking up on me, she sure can be loud when she wants to be. *Screee*. Door opening. *Thunk*. Closing. She doesn't call me for dinner, and I don't check to see if she's made anything. I work my way through the box of crackers on my desk.

Eventually, the sounds stop for the night, and I know my mother has gone to bed.

I brush my teeth, get under my covers, and turn off the light. Shadows quiver behind the window shade, marking the outlines of leaves and tree branches.

And a perched figure.

I squint. Stick legs, a shaggy throat, the curve of a beak. Its head shifts and turns, its beak now lost in the silhouette.

I shiver and roll away onto my side. I close my eyes, but my lids sting. The unsleep is like that. It plays opposites. I try to be still, to relax my body, but then I feel an itch on my leg. I scratch it. Then my ear. I scratch it. Then my forehead. My chin, my elbow, my heel, places I didn't know could itch. I notice the taunt of the clock. *Ticka. Ticka. Ticka.* I even think I hear noises outside, but it's probably the pipes. I wonder how long I've been lying here. An hour? Three hours? More? I must doze off some nights. It would be impossible to exist if I didn't sleep now and then. But I have no memory of sleeping or waking up—not since last summer.

Prickles work up my spine. I can sense the figure still there behind the shade, but I don't want to look. I stick my headphones in my ears. Music can at least block out the sounds of the house, the hum of stillness and waiting. But it can't block out the odors, the stench of staleness and stagnancy. Mel used to ask me, in the early days of our friendship, why I never invited her over. "It's not fair," she'd whine. "We're at my house all the time."

But I couldn't explain. I couldn't tell her what it was

like to come from her pinewood-scented halls to the mustiness my own house stews in. To go from her backyard with its patio and mowed lawn to mine with its weeds and ruins: The greenhouse, cracking and growing things it shouldn't be. The shed, rotting and rusting with junk left by previous residents. The fence, tilting and holding back the woods that lead to who knows where. I told Mel we were better off at her place, and she eventually stopped asking.

Oh, Mel.

Pretty Mel, patient Mel. Always waiting for me on her front steps, playing string games till I came.

Me on my bike, smiling, freewheeling the quarter mile from my house to hers, away from the dead end and the mustiness and my mother, lessons done for the day...

Mel! Mel!

Mel?

The day Mel wasn't there—the day she wasn't waiting for me...

The day seven balloons, all different colors, clung to her front railing, bumping each other in the wind, and the door stood open a sliver...

I nudged the door forward. Voices floated toward me from the kitchen, low and chanting. I followed them on tiptoe, halting at the kitchen doorway and peering into darkness. Orange dots flamed and floated at the center of the room. Cheekbones and nostrils flickered in patches of candlelight. Lips moved, intoning words I couldn't make out. Pointy teeth gleamed, and eyes, dozens of them, reflected the flames.

I screamed.

The lights clicked on, forcing me to blink. A bunch of children blinked back. Mel sat at the head of the table in a cone-shaped paper hat and a dress with puffed sleeves.

"Shh!" Mrs. Asimakos leered at me, her finger to her mouth. I backed away.

Mr. Asimakos rushed to his daughter's side. "It's okay, cupcake. See? It's just Elise. Blow out the candles. Go on. Make a wish."

Mel pouted and shook her head. "My song's ruined." Her lower lip trembled. She erupted with a wail.

I looked around. The room wasn't so scary with the lights on. The candles weren't hovering like I'd thought, but nestled in a cake. And there were colors all around: Streamers and ribbons. Boxes wrapped in shiny paper. More balloons like the ones out front.

"Didn't your mother read the invitation?"

Mrs. Asimakos ushered me to a chair and strapped a cone hat to my head. "The party started an hour ago."

Before I could ask what an invitation was, Mel's wails rose to a painful pitch. Behind her on the wall, a banner glinted with big rainbow words: *Happy 7th Birthday, Melanie!* Mrs. Asimakos cursed and blew out the candles.

When I got home later, I went to my room and took out my dictionary.

birthday | ˈbərθ͵dā | *n. the annual anniversary of the day on which a person was born, typically treated as an occasion for celebration and present-giving.*

I stared at the page until the letters blurred together. "Birthday," I whispered. In the books my mother let me read, the word had never shown up. She'd mentioned my "date of birth" before—that number she writes on forms sometimes— but never "birthday." Never this thing everyone else supposedly celebrated.

I closed the dictionary that day and listened to my mother's footsteps. The shriek of her bedroom door opening. *Screee.* Closing. *Thunk.* I must have done something bad—something unforgiveable—to make her think her only child didn't deserve balloons or cake or presents. To make her hide Mel's invitation. To make her keep me from knowing about birthdays, so she wouldn't have to celebrate mine. I must have done something terrible.

But I couldn't recall what I'd done.

Tap-tap-tap.

My eyes blink open. It's dark. I'm twelve again, lying in bed. By some miracle, I must have nodded off long enough for the music in my headphones to end—and now there's a *tap-tap-tapping* on glass behind me.

I turn over. My eyes adjust to the dark until they can make out my window shade. No silhouette.

I wait for more tapping.

Of course, now that I'm wide awake again, the sound has stopped. I sit up and glare at the shade. Sleep is hard enough to come by. Just when it had finally paid me a visit... just when I had finally drifted off...

A fuse blows inside me. I thrust off my covers and yank up the shade, searching for the mischief maker. The moon casts a glow on the tree by my window, but I see nothing perched there. Just spindly branches against the backyard shapes beyond—the fence, the greenhouse, the shed.

A shadow moving by the shed door.

I squint. It moves again: something taller than what I'm looking for. *Someone* taller? I strain my eyes, but the moonlight shifts, I blink, and then I can't tell shadow from shadow.

I step back from the window, shivering. If I had any hope of falling back asleep, it's history now.

CHAPTER 3

THERE'S NOTHING GREEN-PASTUREY ABOUT Green Pasture Middle School: no grass, no horses, no cows. Just pavement and a parking lot and a squat brick building.

In a way it's nice—the same every morning. The brown doors, the burnt-orange walls, the faces in the halls. No surprises. Once people form an impression of you, that's who you are. Bernard Billows is always going to smell like spoiled milk, and his hair is always going to be long and greasy. The same goes for teachers. If Miss Looping ever stopped wearing those dark velvet dresses or straightened her quivering curls, the whole school would cry doomsday. That's why it's so easy to get by without talking here. At this point, people expect it of me.

I pull my bangs over my penciled eyebrow and take my seat in English class. I glance at Miss Looping's desk, steeling myself for Beady's usual stare.

He isn't there.

I scan the classroom to see if Miss Looping moved him somewhere else, but there's no sign of him. I try not to think anything of it. Maybe she put him in a drawer or took him home. In fact, I hope she did. Good riddance.

I open my notebook, greeted by the torn book page I pasted to the inside cover—the illustration of swans with arching necks and sweeping wings and black knobs on orange bills, and the words wisping across it all:

"Silence is the means of avoiding misfortune. The talkative parrot is shut up in a cage. Other birds, without speech, fly freely about." —*Sakya Pandita*

I know nothing about Sakya Pandita, except that he was some ancient Buddhist scholar. I just like the quote. And the swans. I flip to a blank page and write:

Things could be worse. You could be...

- Shut up in a cage
- Cinderella (before the ball)
- Stranded on a desert island

I gnaw on my pencil and then cross out the last one. On second thought, I wouldn't mind having an island to myself.

There'd be no one expecting me to talk, and I could read all day. As long as I had my book of sonnets, that is. And basic survival skills. Later in the library, I'll have to look up how to build a fire. I should be taking notes—Miss Looping is putting a lot of zest into her Dickens lecture, even drawing a plot diagram of *Oliver Twist* on the board—but I prefer poetry, and I'm on a roll with my list. I add:

- Allergic to chocolate
- On death row
- A fruit fly

"Any questions so far?" Miss Looping gestures at her diagram.

Arty Pilger raises his hand in that way of his that looks like he's screwing in a light bulb.

"Yes, Arty?"

"Your minion's gone." He also has a knack for asking questions that aren't questions.

Miss Looping wipes chalk off her hands. "I meant about Dickens. But yes, Beady went missing yesterday, if that's what you mean. And I was going to announce at the end of class that whoever stole him, and whoever broke my mug, has twenty-four hours to come forward. After that, I'm taking the case to the principal."

The other students look at one another and shrug.

Beady's missing? I slide down in my chair.

"I may have bought him on a whim at a thrift shop," Miss Looping says, "but he's been more to me than a decoration. I expect to see him returned safely."

There's no way this could get traced to me. No one else was in the room at the time. And I didn't do anything wrong. I didn't break the mug, and I didn't steal Beady. I don't know what happened to him. All I know is that I slammed my book shut, and he moved, and I ran, and...

A breeze tickles my neck. I turn to the window Miss Looping always leaves open for "fresh air." An object sits on the windowsill: a feather, jet-black, bluish at an angle.

I jump when the room phone rings.

"Who?" Miss Looping is saying into the phone. "Okay. Right now? Okay." She hangs up. "Elise? You're wanted in the guidance office."

Guidance? I can feel Beady's eyes cackling silently at me, even in his absence. All my classmates' eyes too. I gather my things and shuffle out of the room. I was worried about the principal's office, but guidance sounds ten times worse.

Did Mrs. Bebeau say something to the guidance counselor about me not talking? Or was it Ms. Dively? Miss Looping would never do that to me. I bet it was Mr. Gankle. Or maybe it wasn't a teacher. Maybe it was Sylvia. Or Mel. No, Mel wouldn't do something so mean.

Did they call my mother? What will they make me do? Public-speaking classes? Social activities? But this is a free school—a free country, anyway—and they can't make me do anything. No one calls Bernard Billows to the guidance office to make him take a shower. I won't go. I'll walk straight out the front doors.

But that would be worse. They'll notice I didn't show up, and it will draw even more attention.

They know how to put me in a lose-lose situation.

The door to the office stands open, and the guidance counselor, Ms. Standish, sits at her desk talking. I crane my neck. She's wearing a turtleneck and saying words like *policies* and *assemblies*. I can't see who she's talking to.

She looks up. "Elise. Come on in."

I step in so I can get this over with. A boy and a girl with reddish-brown hair and identical noses sit across from Ms. Standish. Students I've never seen before—here at Green Pasture? Is it possible?

"This is Elise Pileski." Ms. Standish waves at me, and then at the boy and the girl. "Elise, meet Conn and Finola Karney."

"It's Fin." The girl nods at me. "Hey."

The boy nods too and puts his hands in his pockets. Binoculars hang from his neck. Maybe they're a fashion accessory.

I wait for someone to explain why I'm here.

"I was just going to tell them about you," Ms. Standish says. "Conn and Finola are new to Green Pasture. Finola will be joining the seventh grade—"

"It's Fin," the girl repeats.

"—and Conn the eighth grade, like you. They come from a homeschool background, and since you recently made the transition, I thought you could introduce yourself, give advice, answer any questions they might have."

This is the part where I should say something to get myself out of this. Instead I exhale. No one turned me in.

Ms. Standish hands Fin a pamphlet. "That's for you two to share." I glance at the cover: *Transitioning from Homeschool to Public School.* She gave me the same one on my first day. I recognize the picture: kids clutching books and leaning against lockers, mouths open in mid-laugh. No one actually stands like that. It's funny now to think of the images I saw in movies and magazines at Mel's house. Lunch ladies in hairnets. Teachers with apples. White chalk against clean blackboards. Students in rows at graffiti-free desks, hands raised in eagerness.

I should probably warn Fin and Conn so they won't be disappointed. But that would require speaking, and they'll see the reality soon enough.

Ms. Standish glances at her watch. "I have to run to a meeting. Shall I leave you to it?" She stands and frowns. "May I ask why you're wearing those?" She points at Conn's binoculars.

"Oh." Fin waves a hand. "He wears them everywhere."

Ms. Standish presses the tips of her fingers together. "Well, you'll need to take them off while you're in the building. Other students might find them distracting."

"Distracting?" Conn snorts. "Why would they be—"

"Just do it." Fin nudges him.

He rolls his eyes and shoves the binoculars in his backpack. "*How* unnecessary," he mutters, drawing out the *how*. Ms. Standish doesn't seem to hear. Fin grins and presses her lips together. Conn shakes his head and looks at the ceiling. After a second, he grins too.

I've always been curious about siblings. I used to study Mel and her sister, the way they fought over every little thing, but then her sister moved away to college. These two interest me even more. Not just their matching hair and noses, but the way they interact. The way they exchange glances and elbow each other and snicker at nothing, communicating in their brother-sister language. A language I'll never speak.

Conn notices me staring and coughs. "So, any advice?"

I look around and realize Ms. Standish has left. Should I bolt now or try to stick it out for a minute? Bolting now would be wisest.

But Fin and Conn are waiting for me to answer. And as I stand here, I see that I'm at an advantage. They don't know about me yet. They have no expectations. To them, I could be anyone. I could be the most talkative person in the school, in the world. I could be—what's the word?—*outgoing*, like Sylvia. I haven't proven otherwise yet. I'm a blank slate.

I don't know if it's this thought or the way they're staring that makes my mouth open. "Are you twins?"

I cringe at my words. They don't even answer Conn's question. And now today's tally is shot. So much for zero.

"Us?" Fin laughs. "Nah, we're a year apart. I just turned twelve, and he's thirteen. People always say we look alike, though."

"But I'm the better-looking one, right?" Conn peers sidelong at me.

I feign interest in my shoelaces. He's right, but I'm not about to tell him that.

Fin waves a hand. "Ignore Mister Big Head over here. What about you? Any obnoxious siblings?"

I shake my head.

"You're an only child?" Her eyes widen. "What's it like? Do your parents buy you everything you want?" She leans forward, her freckles bold.

Conn elbows her.

"What?" She elbows him back. "I've always wanted to be an only child. Be spoiled, get all the attention. It must be nice."

I twist the strings on my sweatshirt. I decide not to tell Fin that I'm a stranger to being spoiled. That she just confirmed my mother's indifference.

"So, why'd you make the switch to public school?" Conn is looking at me again.

Open-ended questions should be against the law.

"Sorry." Conn clears his throat. "I know it's a personal question. You don't have to—"

"I wanted a change," I blurt out, surprising myself

again. Four more words. I'm getting farther from zero when I ought to be getting closer. I need to get out of here.

"Sounds like us." Fin pulls up her legs and sits cross-legged in her chair. "And your folks were okay with it?"

At least this answer is yes or no. I nod, because nodding won't add to my tally. And nodding is easier than forming words, easier than trying to explain what I still don't understand myself. How I'd been asking for months if I could enroll in public school, how I'd reached a sort of boiling point, sick of longing to be part of Mel's school stories, and even sicker of my mother's halfhearted lessons. But each time I asked, my mother made some remark about how she didn't approve of public schools.

Then that day in July, when she said she was "disappointed" in my latest exam score—88 percent—my anger flared up. And I made that comment. *You should have had more kids then. Maybe they wouldn't have disappointed you.* It wasn't a fair comeback, I know—my father had obviously died before they could have more kids—but I was seething. She didn't reply. There was that flash in her eyes, though. And the next morning, I found her waiting at the kitchen table. *I called Green Pasture*, she said, smoothing out the already-smooth tablecloth. *You'll start September 1st. And I'll finally have more time for other things.* I stood there in disbelief. I'd gotten what I wanted. But somehow it felt more like a punishment than a conquest.

"You're lucky." Conn shakes his head. "Our folks weren't so easily convinced."

Fin grunts. "They're *still* not convinced. I mean, they only caved because we kept threatening them."

I lift my eyebrows in spite of myself. Conn sits up. "Oh, she just means we threatened to run away. It was part of our protest. And it exploded into this nasty fight."

"A fight we should have had sooner." Fin huffs. "Now it's late in the year, probably too late to join a team. I really wanted to do softball." She turns to me. "Do you think I missed the boat?"

I shake my head. She'll hear about the principal's everybody-has-to-join-one-thing initiative on the intercom. No need for me to tell her too. I eye the door as the itch grows itchier. I'm in risky territory. The longer I stay here, the higher my chances are of being asked more questions, of adding too much to my tally, of saying something regrettable.

"Gotta pee." The lie escapes me. I turn and leave without waiting for a response.

I slip out the door that cuts through the courtyard—if

you can even call it a courtyard. It's more like a square of cracked pavement in the center of the school, with a birch tree and a couple of benches. Whoever named Green Pasture Middle School didn't name it after the courtyard. I don't know *what* they named it after. I walk across the empty square toward the other door. Fin and Conn will probably tell Ms. Standish I ditched them, but that's a price I'll have to pay.

Something whooshes by my neck. I duck and look up. The sky gapes, gray. I rub my neck and keep walking.

As I approach the door, leaves on the birch tree rustle. My eyes swivel toward the tree, squinting. It takes me a minute to distinguish leaves from feathers. Then I see it: a bird posted on the highest branch, watching me. It's entirely black, from its bowie knife of a beak down to its stick legs. I blink. More rustling. Then I see only leaves again.

I rub the goose bumps on my arms and hurry inside.

CHAPTER 4

I HEAD TO SCIENCE CLASS early and take my place in the back row. Bernard Billows dozes in the front. I doodle in my notebook as other students trickle in. Someone takes out scissors and snips off a piece of Bernard Billows's hair.

Mr. Gankle strolls in and sets his briefcase on his desk. The scissors retreat. "I assume everyone read the chapter I assigned?"

Nods ripple across the room.

"Good." Mr. Gankle leans back against his desk. "Well, instead of me lecturing and droning on about it, today we're going to have a class discussion."

My body reacts on cue: heart starts to pound, pulse quickens, dread rises from the pit of my stomach. As inevitable as flinching at a whip or squinting in the sun. I run my pencil over a line in my notebook until the paper tears.

"So what did we learn in this chapter? Who wants to start?"

Silence. People shift in their seats.

I relax. No one did the reading except for me. *Sorry, Mr. Gankle, no discussion today. What a shame.*

"Do I need to give a pop quiz?" He crosses his arms.

A throat clears. Everyone turns to look at Arty Pilger, who's infamous for failing pop quizzes. He pushes his red-framed glasses up his nose. "The chapter's about cells."

A girl in the back snickers.

"Genius," someone mutters.

I draw squiggly shapes in my notebook. See, I know better than Arty Pilger. He's a case in point: *Silence is the means of avoiding misfortune.* Better to stay silent. Sakya Pandita was a genius, not Arty.

Mr. Gankle sighs. "Okay... Can anyone be more specific?" He drums his fingers on his desk. "Remember, participation is worth forty percent of your grade."

Hands fly up.

I listen as, one by one, students cross over to the other side. The side where people are safe. Free. Off the hook. My ears catch words like *cytoplasm, organelle, nucleus.* Mr. Gankle is nodding and jotting the words on the board with his dry-erase marker. Soon, almost everyone in the room has crossed over. Some have crossed over more than once.

Only one person is left on my side. I glance over at

Bernard Billows, who stares out the window, tapping his construction boots against the floor. As long as he stays on my side, I'm okay. Even if he *is* Bernard Billows and he smells funny and his hair is greasy, he still counts as a person in the room. Strength in numbers.

I should probably say something, though. Participation is forty percent.

Participation. What does that even mean? According to my pocket dictionary, *participate* means "to take part." It doesn't say "to talk." But according to Mr. Gankle—according to most teachers—that's what it means. Even Albert Einstein would fail this class if he didn't "participate."

The minutes inch by. Five, then ten. I try to think of something to say, something that hasn't already been said. It's hard to think with everybody talking. I'll just say something simple. It doesn't need to be brilliant or interesting. It just needs to be something so I can cross to the other side and be done with it. It will feel good to be done with it.

"Mr. Gankle?" The construction boots stop tapping.

"Go ahead."

I hate you, Bernard Billows.

"There was an interesting bit about the membrane. How it acts as this sort of filter, separating the inside of the cell from its outside environment..." He goes on in his slow, emphatic way, summarizing membrane facts as if he's memorized them. I knew he would say something eventually. He always does. Everyone does. And I remain, the last one standing.

"Who hasn't contributed yet? Have we heard from everyone?"

I fix my eyes on my notebook, but I can sense Mr. Gankle scanning the room as if he's trying to sniff out a criminal. My body turns to stone—a reflex no one but me seems to have. But maybe it's a good thing. If I act enough like a statue, Mr. Gankle's eyes will skip over me.

This logic always makes sense in the moment.

"Elise, we haven't heard from you yet. What can you tell us about cells?"

Mr. Gankle is looking at me now, his dry-erase marker waiting in his hand. The other students stare at their laps or their desks like I'm a bad movie they can't bring themselves to watch. I try to open my mouth, but it's frozen shut. The seconds pass. Anyone would think my brain doesn't work, that nothing's happening in my head, but that's not true because my mind is racing a thousand miles a minute. It never rests. It gives me headaches.

I prepare to live out eternity at this desk, inside this bubble, this membrane.

"*Aaaa-choo!*" Someone sneezes: Arty.

"Bless you," the class choruses, and attention shifts away. The bell rings. My classmates spring out of their seats.

I sit still as the room empties.

Eventually, my fingers move to my notebook, flipping past the quote with the swans and through pages and pages of tally marks. The notebook is nearly full. My tally's as low as ever.

So why am I still doing it? The plan had been to...

I clamp my eyes shut, trying to remember. Yes, there had been a plan. Back in September. After I sat down in my first class, algebra. Ms. Dively asked us what the quadratic formula was. I smiled and recited it—I'd learned that one years ago. Ms. Dively narrowed her eyes at me and said something about the hand-raising rule. I didn't know about hand-raising then. It was something I never had to do in home lessons, and Mel had failed to warn me about it. I resolved to be more careful in my next class.

But Mr. Scroggins, it turned out, didn't care about hand-raising; he called on people. He asked me to read a paragraph aloud from our textbook. I cleared my throat, thinking this was my chance to redeem myself. Forget Ms. Dively. After I read three sentences, someone laughed. Mr. Scroggins smiled at me and said, "It's pronounced 'mis-hap,' not 'mish-ap.'" It occurred to me there might be other words I didn't know how to pronounce.

Moments like these accumulated. They gathered like clouds throughout the morning, threatening a downpour.

When the lunch bell rang, I exhaled. I would get to see Mel. She was saving me a seat. I was still mad that Green Pasture had made me take that placement test and put me a year ahead, but at least Mel and I could have lunch together, even if we weren't in the same grade.

I found her in the cafeteria at a crowded table. They were all looking at me—Sylvia and Nellie and Theresa, whose faces I didn't know yet but whose names I knew from Mel's stories. Mel introduced me, and even though my stomach was fluttering a little, I smiled as widely as I could. All summer, I'd heard Mel talk about her newest "school friends." Now that my mother didn't want to homeschool me anymore, I'd get to be one of them.

I still remember the first thing Sylvia said.

"There's something in your teeth."

Mel nudged her.

"There is?" I panicked, running my tongue along my incisors.

"It was just a pepper flake or something." Mel did a sort of giggle. "I think it's gone now." Then she frowned at Sylvia.

"Oh." I forced a laugh. Had it been there all morning for everyone to see?

"How'd you like your first classes?" It was Nellie who changed the subject. "Are your teachers complete weirdos like mine?"

I smiled again, and then clamped my lips shut. I had to be careful about showing my teeth in case I had more food stuck there. I decided I should say something funny back to start off on the right foot. Mel's friends were my friends now. "Ms. Dively was all right," I said. "Kind of a drag. But Mr. Scroggins..." I shuddered for effect. "His voice sounds like a vacuum machine. And have you seen his bow tie? Who told him that was a good idea?"

I waited, but Nellie didn't laugh. No one did. She and the others exchanged glances.

At my right, Theresa shifted. "He's my dad."

My face went hot.

Theresa got up and walked across the cafeteria to the vending machine.

Sylvia grinned. "Well, that was awkward." Her grin surprised me. Did she really find amusement in her friend's embarrassment? But if she was grinning, maybe what I'd done wasn't that bad.

I looked at my untouched sandwich. "I didn't know."

Mel waved a hand. "She'll get over it. Theresa can't stay mad at anyone for long."

"You think so?"

"Yeah, yeah. She'll forget by tomorrow."

But Theresa didn't forget. At lunch the next day, she gave me the coldest of cold shoulders.

Mel tried to ease the tension. "So, Elise," she chirped. "I showed everyone that rhyme you wrote for my birthday last month. It was a hit."

"Oh, right, the one about a shooting star?" Sylvia said through a mouthful of fries. "It was cute. You should be a poet."

"Really? Thank you." I'd been going for "moving" rather than "cute," but it was still a nice thing to hear; I'd never thought of myself as good at anything, least of all poetry. And I was just grateful that not all of Mel's friends hated me after my mishap—*mis-hap*—yesterday. I wanted to keep the goodwill going and say something nice back to Sylvia, something thoughtful and personal. "Sorry to hear your dad left, by the way," I said. "That must have been tough. Are you doing okay?"

"Elise," Mel said between her teeth.

"Wait, what?" Nellie's head whipped toward Sylvia.

"Your dad left, Sylv?" Theresa's eyes widened. "When?"

Sylvia's cheeks burned scarlet. "A couple of weeks ago. It's no big deal." She glowered at Mel. "I was gonna tell the rest of you soon."

Mel wrung her napkin. "I didn't think Elise would say anything."

"Whatever. It's fine." Sylvia stood.

Mel stood too. "I didn't tell anyone else, I swear."

"I have to pee." Sylvia grabbed her bag and walked off.

Mel shot me a glare—she'd never glared at me before—and then hurried after Sylvia, leaving me alone with Nellie and Theresa, who were already speculating and gossiping about Sylvia's parents.

My body went rigid, my tongue dry. What was going on? Every time I opened my mouth, things got worse instead of better. It had never been like this at home or at Mel's house. But here at school, my voice was a ticking bomb, each tick sending me closer to ruin. If things went on this way, I'd make enemies of everyone.

I couldn't stand the thought of being Mel's enemy.

I said nothing for the remainder of lunch and sat in the

back row for all of my classes. When teachers called my name for attendance, my heart started thumping and my muscles tensed, but I pushed out a "here." When someone asked me for the time, I managed "one-thirty." When someone asked if I had a pencil they could borrow, I muttered "sure." I said only what was necessary. It was better that way. I was less likely to speak out of turn or mispronounce a word or insult someone's father or spill the beans.

That was the same day I started tallying.

In the week that followed, the heart thumping and body stiffening got worse, but I found shortcuts. When teachers took attendance, I just raised my hand. When someone asked me for the time, I just showed them my watch. When someone asked if I had a pencil, I just shook my head. I decided to use these shortcuts for a few more days, another week at most— just until I learned how things worked at Green Pasture. Just until I got things under control. It was the perfect plan.

I close my notebook now and glance at Mr. Gankle's *Science Rocks!* calendar, with its monthly photo of geologists holding rocks. It's April fifth—well into the second semester. I've learned how things work. I know public school inside and out. So it's time to stop. Isn't it?

Why can't I stop?

CHAPTER 5

TURN MY BIKE OFF the main road and start up the hill past Mel's house.

I check her bedroom window, top right, but the blinds are closed.

Just months ago, I might have found her waiting for me on the front steps. Just months ago, I would have felt welcome here—more welcome than in my own house. Now I feel welcome in neither. Funny.

I push on up the hill, my calf muscles burning. I don't know why we have to live all the way up at the edge of town. Even though the nearest house—Mel's—is only a minute's bike ride away, or two when I'm going uphill, my house still feels so much more *apart*. Maybe because it's almost in the woods. If it weren't for the fence holding back the trees, the woods would swallow the house right up. I keep pumping until I see the two oak trees shrouding the front of the house. The overgrown grass. The peeling paint. The woods encroaching from behind. Home sweet home.

The station wagon is gone, and I remember it's Thursday. My mother goes to the town library on Mondays and Thursdays to do work for the online class she's teaching. I toss my bike against the fence and head inside. It feels like a vacation every time—not having to answer to her on my way past the kitchen.

Halfway down the hall, I pause. My mother's door is open a crack.

I stare at the opening. Usually she's so careful. She must have been in a rush.

Light flickers through the gap: sunshine maybe, filtering through the windows that must be in there. Almost thirteen years living in this house with her, and I've never set foot in her bedroom. I've seen glimpses of it while passing down the hall as she was coming in or out: a dresser, a lamp, the same brown carpet that runs through the hall and every room upstairs. Nothing of interest. But I've never been inside before. The door is always closed, even when she's out. Even when she's down the hall or in the bathroom. I tried opening it twice while she was in the shower—first when I was five or six, and again a few years ago. Both times it was locked. I assumed, after that, that she always locked it. It's something she would do.

But the door is open now, and she's not home.

I nudge the wood with my finger. It creaks forward. I step inside and brace myself—for what, I don't know.

A nightstand. A closet. A mirror. Ordinary. Boring. Curtains flutter at an open window, where towels hang out to dry. The bed is made up, with six tasseled pillows resting against the headboard in a geometric arrangement. The comforter is pulled tight, free of wrinkles. I gawk. Does she do this every day? Does she really put all this care into making a bed that no one but her ever sees? I never make my bed.

I open the closet: a bunch of clothes, long out of fashion. I turn to the dresser and open the top drawer: underwear. I wrinkle my nose and move to the second drawer: T-shirts. Third drawer: stockings. Fourth: nightgowns. Predictable. Everything you'd expect to find.

She does it to spite me then. Why else would she keep her door closed all the time? She has nothing to hide. Nothing embarrassing or criminal or even personal. She shuts me out for the sake of shutting me out.

I shove the drawer into place and look back at the bed.

I don't know if it's the pillow arrangement or the tautness of the comforter that gives me the urge to jump on it. To demolish that perfect handiwork.

No. If I'm going to do any damage, it should be subtle. Just enough to disturb the peace without giving me away.

I lift a corner of the comforter and tear the seam a little.

A thrill ripples through me.

I kneel and lift the bed skirt, finding a couple of shoeboxes. I pull one out and open it. A layer of electric bills and tax forms lies on top. I sift through; nothing but forms all the way to the bottom. I pull out the other box. More of the same. Water bills. Invoices. Envelopes addressed to my mother.

Near the bottom, I notice one envelope with my name. A square one, blue. I pick it out. The postmark date is almost nine years ago. The zip code in the return address is only two numbers off from ours. The envelope has been torn open. I pull out the card inside, a greeting card with a lion cub and the number four on the front.

I heard somebody's turning four… I open the card. *So I'm sending you a loving ROAR!*

Faded handwriting follows the rhyme:

Happy Birthday, Elise! A little something for your college fund.

Love,
Granny P

Granny P? The P must stand for Pileski, but my mother has never mentioned her. Then again, she never mentions any relatives. She doesn't speak to them for whatever reason, and they don't speak to her. By the looks of it, though, they've tried to speak to me. At least one has. Granny P must have given up on a granddaughter she never heard from.

Tucked in the card is a hundred-dollar bill with a tear at the corner. Of course. That's the only reason my mother stashed this card. She cares about the money, not my birthday. She must have forgotten about this bill, or else she surely would have spent it by now.

I close the card and slip it back in the envelope. I can see how hard my mother tried. She really, really tried to cover all the bases. No birthday cards in the mail. No family contact. No television. No public school. No access to the internet or her password-protected laptop. But she messed up. She let me be friends with Mel, that day when Mrs. Asimakos came to our door with cookies, a new-to-the-area smile, and a daughter my height. My mother saw no choice but to let them in.

After their half-hour visit, she told me I could go to Mel's house some days after lessons. Mrs. Asimakos wouldn't mind, she said, and it would be good for me to play with someone my own age. She must have been pretty desperate to get me out of the house, desperate enough to accept the risk that Mel might introduce me to things she'd been keeping from me—television, the internet, public school. Birthday parties.

She must know I've figured it out by now. Could that be one reason she let me go to public school—she realized there was no point in trying to keep birthdays from me anymore? She's still never mentioned them, never said the word *birthday* in my presence. She pretends that neither of us knows the concept, and because she pretends, I pretend. And we go on pretending. I put Granny P's card back in the envelope. Who knows how many other birthday cards have come for me over the years, long since recycled? The thought makes my teeth scrape together. I reach for the box to check for more cards, but a car door slams outside.

I spring to my feet. Through my mother's window I can see the station wagon in the driveway.

And a black feather on the sill, like the one at Miss Looping's window.

The front door *screees* open. I shove all the papers and envelopes back into the shoebox, except for Granny P's card. I slip that beneath my shirt. Then I push the box under the bed and skid out of the room and down the hall. I hear my mother slinking up the stairs—see her foot on the landing—as I slip around the corner into my room, onto my bed, just in time.

Just in time to realize I left her door wide open.

CHAPTER 6

Things could be worse. You could be...

- Homeless
- Covered with acne
- A peasant in the Middle Ages

LIFT MY PENCIL AND admire how long my list is getting. My tally has been staying at zero all day so far, so I need something else to work on. I think for a minute, then add:

- Stuck in quicksand
- On crutches with a broken leg
- In trouble for snooping in your mother's room

I've managed to avoid my mother since yesterday, and she hasn't mentioned anything—yet—about her door being open. Maybe I've lucked out and she thinks she left it open herself. At the same time, I want her to see the ripped seam. I want her to know I found the card. I want her to know…

The lunch bell interrupts my thoughts. I close my notebook and get up off the toilet before other girls start pouring in. At least I don't have to go back to French class. Mrs. Bebeau wanted us to practice conversational French for the last five minutes, so I grabbed a bathroom pass like my life depended on it. I should probably return the pass now, but Mrs. Bebeau might still be in the room when I get there. I decide to leave it in the stall "by accident."

As I emerge from the bathroom, the air rumbles with voices and the scratching of Styrofoam lunch trays. Students with flyers hover outside the cafeteria doors, and most days I'm quick enough to get by unscathed, but one girl pounces, shoving a flyer in my face. "Hey there, join our team!" I take the flyer so she'll leave me alone and stuff it in my bag without looking at it. I hustle away and turn left toward the library, passing Miss Looping's classroom. The door is closed, but I peek in the window at Miss Looping's desk—where Beady should be but hasn't been for two days now. I wonder if Miss Looping has told the principal yet. What will he do? Will he even care? He must have bigger things to worry about than a missing stuffed bird.

I walk on, maybe a little too fast, until the familiar double doors and sign come into view. QUIET IN THE LIBRARY. I like knowing there are some things I can count on, like these block letters and lunch with Bernard Billows and the librarian.

"Elise."

I hear my name before I reach the doors.

I halt and turn. Mel is walking toward me. Why isn't she at lunch? At least Sylvia and the others aren't with her.

"I wanted to see if you joined a team or club yet," she says.

I hesitate. It's not a question, technically. It doesn't warrant a response, technically.

"I was thinking of trying track. There's an open practice after school today. Maybe it could be something for us to do together."

I adjust the straps on my backpack. Mel and I used to race each other in her backyard for fun. We'd joke that we were training for the Olympics, when really we just wanted to feel our hearts hammering. I never thought about running on a team.

"And maybe tomorrow, if you're not doing anything, we could go for milk shakes or something. Hang out."

She wants me to do track with her and get milk shakes. Maybe I'm still her best friend. Maybe I should go along.

"Sylvia's having a sleepover later that night. You're invited to that too."

Why does she have to ruin it?

I don't know why she likes Sylvia. She talks too loud and has mascara clumps and makes fun of the lunch ladies.

"Can you come?" Mel crosses her arms, waiting. "Come on. You're not going to sit at home on a Saturday night, are you?"

I keep adjusting my backpack straps until they're too tight.

She shakes her head. "I don't get it. You used to talk all the time at my house. What happened?"

I let go of the straps. I want to prove her wrong, to tell her that she's lost it and nothing's changed and I'm the same as before. That she's the crazy one, not me. That she's the one who acts different at school. Since when does she care so much about being part of a group? Even here in the hall, just us, she isn't the Mel I know, the Mel who used to say she'd rather have one close friend than a hundred acquaintances. I see right through this fake Mel, this "school Mel." I'd like to tell her that.

But if I talk to her here and not at lunch, she'll make a big deal out of it. She'll never stop asking questions. I made that mistake before, during the second week of school, when she came up to me in the courtyard, just her. No one else was around, and it felt like we were hanging out on her front steps again, and my muscles loosened and my throat opened and the bubble popped and I started talking like I used to. I don't know why the bubble pops when I'm alone with her. It's selective like that.

I could go that route again now, talk to Mel, tell her what I found in my mother's room yesterday. Ask her if she's met the new kids, Fin and Conn, or if she thinks a stuffed bird could fly out a window.

But if I want to curb people's questions, I need to be consistent. Because I know what they're thinking: If I can speak at one point, shouldn't I be able to speak at any point? It's only logical.

But nothing about this feels logical. I've been telling myself it started as a choice, a plan, back in September...but what about the heart thumping and the muscle stiffening and the throat tightening? The bubble? I didn't plan for *that*. How can I tell Mel that this is feeling more and more like a force beyond my control? She'd never buy it. No one would. That's why I have to be consistent. It's the only way to stop the questions.

At the same time, I want Mel to stop looking at me like that.

I wipe my forehead. I could always shrug again. That's a good fallback.

But with the way she's staring at me, I suspect a shrug won't satisfy her.

"Just tell me, Elise. Why are you so quiet all the time?"

That word.

She won't stop looking at me. How can I make her stop? There's only one way. I have to say something just this once, so her eyes will stop drilling through my head.

"I have nothing to say," I blurt out. There. That should appease her. At least she can't argue with that.

I wonder if my words are true.

"Nothing to say?" She frowns. "It's been, like, seven months since school started. You've had nothing to say for seven months?"

Consistency. Be consistent.

"Forget it." She throws up her hands and turns away. "I'm done."

I study the ground, listening to her footsteps fade. I'm not sure what troubles me more: that everyone wants an explanation from me, or that I don't have one.

I sit in the library and stare at my notebook. People want to know why I don't talk. So do I. I almost wish I'd experienced some traumatic event, or lost a loved one, or been physically abused or something, just so I could have an excuse. Like in those novels in the library, with descriptions like "So-and-so hasn't said a word since the earthquake took her family," or "After watching his twin fall from a cliff, So-and-so won't speak to anyone." Heck, I'd even take the little mermaid's excuse—that I made a bargain with a sea witch.

But I've never met a sea witch. And the most traumatic event I've experienced was a bee sting. And the only "loved one" I've lost was my father, when I was too young to remember him or understand what it means to be killed by a drunk driver. And no one has ever laid a hand on me.

I open my notebook and count on my fingers: *I, have, nothing, to, say.* I scratch down five tally marks. I stare at them and chew on my pencil until I taste metal.

The nice thing about zero marks is that your mind has no words to cling to, to shudder at, to regret, to replay over and over in your head. But now these five words will replay over and over for the rest of the day, the rest of the night.

I put my notebook back in my bag, finding the flyer I stuffed there. I uncrumple it.

Got pent-up energy? The track team needs more runners!

I nibble on a hangnail. Track. Running. If I have to join

something, maybe I wouldn't mind track. Mel might be there. And if I run every day, maybe I'll be so exhausted by bedtime that I'll actually sleep. And if being on the track team can keep me busy, distracted, maybe the rest of the school year will go by faster. Because right now it's taking forever.

The first thing I learn at track practice is that Green Pasture has the worst track team in the league. Coach Ewing doesn't show her teeth when she tells me this, so I'm guessing she's not too proud. But she says I might as well know.

"Hmm, you're small." She looks me up and down. "What event do you wanna run?"

I shrug.

"Are you a sprinter or a distance runner?"

I shrug again.

"A woman of few words, eh? We'll train you for the mile race to start."

I find myself in a clump of girls, running once around the track and then out onto a road that leads through quiet neighborhoods, led by one of the co-captains, Beverly. Mel's in the clump too. She joined the team after all. So did Sylvia, Nellie, and Theresa. I shouldn't be surprised. Mel can't do anything without that group now. When she said track was something we could "do together," of course she didn't mean just the two of us. And now that I'm on the team with her, she hasn't so much as glanced my way.

Forget it. I'm done. Maybe she meant it.

But it's fine, it's okay. It's no reason to quit when I've barely started. Besides, there's no talking here. Everyone is concentrating so hard on breathing in and out, trying not to wheeze too loudly or fall behind, willing themselves to keep moving even though they want to collapse and curl up like babies.

It turns out Fin is on the track team too—she must have changed her mind about softball—but she isn't doing the three-mile run with us distance runners. As we left the track, I spotted her doing shot put and javelin with the throwers. And as we jogged by the soccer field, I saw Conn practicing with the soccer team. I guess neither of them put off joining something like I did.

In through the nose, out through the mouth. That's how Coach Ewing said we should breathe. And don't swing your arms from side to side. That's bad form. Keep them moving straight, forward and backward. Don't make fists. That causes tension. Relax your hands, and touch your thumbs to your middle fingers. After the first mile, everyone except me seems to forget these things. Even the two eighth graders who flew past us all in the first minute are lagging now. I heard someone whisper that they're sprinters and that sometimes they join the long-distancers to show off. But now it looks like they've used up all their energy while the rest of us, or at least most of us, have saved some for the last two miles.

I decide that I like track. It's an individual's sport. None of that teamwork like in soccer or basketball or field hockey, where you have to call out to your teammates and work together and rely on other people to pass you the ball. In track, I'm my own team. Me and my legs and my lungs. And my thoughts.

At first I don't know if I should pass people, even though the sprinters did. But some girls are going so slow that I'll be stuck behind them forever if I don't pass. So I breathe in deeply and overtake one girl, and then another. As I pass Mel, I think she hates me a little more. But that feeling of passing someone, sweeping by them, makes me feel like I'm going somewhere, making progress. It assures me I'm not running in place.

"Jeez," one girl huffs behind me. "For someone so short, you're surprisingly fast."

I guess she's right that it's surprising. I have to work harder than the long-legged girls.

But I already know what it's like to work harder than others to do something that comes easily to them. I think of the cafeteria, the class discussions, the bubble—and then I run a little faster.

CHAPTER 7

'M IN NO RUSH to see my mother, so I take the long way home through downtown. I bike past the bank and the post office and the Laundromat, slowing in front of the new pastry shop. Sticky buns, croissants, and muffins fill the window. The scent of bread and cinnamon tugs at my nostrils. My stomach rumbles. I guess track practice can work up an appetite. I peer through the glass. Patsy's Pastries doesn't look busy—there's a woman browsing and a clerk sorting scones behind the counter—so I lock my bike to a rack at the corner and go inside. I head for the counter, but a display case catches my eye. I move toward it, scanning all of the cakes organized by occasion: weddings, baby showers, graduations, christenings, bat mitzvahs, bar mitzvahs. Birthdays.

I pause at the birthday cakes. In front, a Barbie doll's torso rises out of a half-dome cake. Across the gown, ribbons of icing spell out *Happy Birthday, Princess!* I wonder if this one is chocolate or vanilla. Not that I remember the difference.

I haven't tasted cake since Mel's tenth birthday party, the last one I ever went to. Mel eventually forgave me for ruining her seventh birthday—it doesn't take long to forgive at seven years old—so I snuck to her next couple of birthday parties. But Mel's school friends, the ones she had before Sylvia and the gang, started to get on my nerves, giggling about things that happened at "recess" or "gym class" and making fun of teachers I didn't know. And Mel kept asking why I went to her birthday parties but never invited her to mine. So I stopped going. And I told her the truth, because I hated lying to her.

"She doesn't celebrate birthdays at all?" Mel gaped. "Not even her own?"

"As far as I know."

Mel thought for a minute and then brightened. "Maybe she's a Jehovah's Witness."

"A *what*?"

"I have a family friend who's one. They don't celebrate birthdays."

For a magical moment I thought that I'd found the answer—that my mother's birthday avoidance wasn't about me at all.

Then Mel mentioned that Jehovah's Witnesses are some

kind of religious sect. My mother isn't religious. I still remember the day a pair of missionaries came to our door and asked her if she believed in God. "Once upon a time," she replied, and shut the door in their faces.

I glance at the other customer in the shop: a woman in a business suit, about my mother's age, looking at a Sweet Sixteen cake. I try to picture my mother in a business suit. I can't. I try to picture her here in Patsy's Pastries buying me a cake. I can't.

"What can I get you?"

I look up.

The clerk is smiling at me across the counter. It's such a simple thing, ordering a muffin. And yet, here I am looking at the shelf of pastries behind him, tilting my head like I'm still deciding.

"How about one of our sticky buns? They're fresh out of the oven."

I nod. I wanted a muffin, but this is easier. And the sticky buns do look tasty. He picks a bun off the shelf and rings me up. I fish some money out of my pocket. "Enjoy," he says, and then goes off to help the businesswoman. I don't look back at the doll cake.

As I turn and bite into the sweet dough, I think, *This is happiness.*

"Hey, Elise."

I jump a foot in the air, and my happiness drops to the ground.

"Whoops... Shoot... Sorry."

I look up, finding myself at eye level with a pair of binoculars.

"I'll buy you another one." Conn darts around me to the cash register before I can object with a head shake or a hand gesture. I watch him call the clerk and point to the sticky buns. He takes out his wallet. I could flee while his back is turned—there's still time. But that would make me a jerk. And I want a sticky bun.

Conn approaches with two paper bags and hands me one. "Sorry about that."

I smile, which is close enough to a thank-you, and start to turn toward the door, toward safety...

"Are you doing anything right now?"

...but not fast enough. I race to think of an excuse. I could have a test to study for or a dentist appointment or—

"Let's sit a minute." He doesn't wait for me to respond, just strolls over to a table and sits. He bites into his bun and waves at the chair next to him.

I stand there about five seconds and realize I've missed

my window—the one to two seconds after someone addresses me, in which I need to acknowledge what they said or pretend I didn't hear. It's crucial to act within this window. If I hesitate, it's impossible to pull off the pretending. If I wait too long, it's awkward. Right now it's both. I have no choice but to sit.

I join Conn's table and take a huge bite out of my bun. Does the tally still apply after school? This is new territory. No Green Pasture kids have ever tried to talk to me outside of school—mainly because I tend not to go places where I might encounter them. It doesn't matter; we'll be so busy eating that there won't be a chance to talk. I'll keep my mouth full the whole time. It's rude to talk with your mouth full.

"You never came back from the bathroom the other day," Conn says with his mouth full. So much for that. "Fin scare you off?"

I shake my head and keep chewing.

"There's this new bird documentary playing at the cinema tomorrow night. It sounds interesting."

A bird documentary? Not that there are many "interesting" things to do in this town, but a documentary wouldn't have been my first thought.

"I thought I might check it out. If you want to come."

I chew as slowly as possible. I'm running out of bites.

The bread is dissolving on my tongue, and soon I'm going to have to swallow.

He clears his throat. "We could get pizza after. I heard that place on Main Street is good."

I guess he hasn't been at Green Pasture long enough. He still doesn't know about me. We don't have any classes together, so he doesn't realize I'm the last person he should associate with, after Bernard Billows. The feeling I had in Ms. Standish's office comes flooding back: a blank slate. No preconceptions. No adjective attached to me.

It tempts me.

"I know tomorrow's Saturday, so you probably have plans."

My throat sucks the last bits down. My mouth empties.

You're not going to sit at home on a Saturday night, are you?

I look down at my bun. Maybe it wouldn't so bad to go see a film and have pizza. I do like pizza.

"No," I hear myself say.

Conn frowns a little.

"No plans," I mumble.

"Oh." He smiles hesitantly. "Cool."

I'm not sure if I just agreed to go tomorrow or not. I don't think he's sure either.

"Why are you wearing those?" I blurt out. The question comes out sharper than I meant, though I didn't mean for it to come out at all. I need to keep my mouth shut if I know what's good for me.

"Wearing what?"

I point at his binoculars.

He shrugs. "Why not?"

I raise an eyebrow.

"What can I say? I'm a man of mystery."

"And alliteration." Oops.

He raises an eyebrow back at me. "What are you, a poet or something?"

I bite into my bun to stop a smile. Maybe this isn't so hard. We're having a conversation. Like it used to be with Mel. Maybe I could ask him if he likes poetry, or what his favorite ice cream flavor is, or if he thinks it's possible for an inanimate object to fly out a window…

"Yo, Connie boy."

We look up. Two girls have come into the shop. I recognize Fin right away. I identify the other girl as they approach. I don't know her name, but she's a seventh grader like Fin and Mel, and she's on the track team—one of the hurdlers. I've seen her in the girls' bathroom a couple of times too. She's someone who would know enough about me. Someone who would have an adjective attached to me.

Conn nods at Fin. "Look who the cat dragged in."

"We saw you in the window."

"That's not creepy at all. You remember Elise, right?"

"You think my memory's that bad?" She waves a hand at the girl trailing her. "This is Dawn. We have some classes together."

Dawn raises her hand to the level of her hips and twitches it in a lazy wave.

"Want to join us?" Conn says.

"Sure."

Fin and Dawn each pull up a chair. I take another bite of my sticky bun, but it's lost some of its flavor.

Fin plops down in her chair and eyes Conn's bun. "That's making my mouth water." She holds out a hand. "Let me have a bite, Connie boy."

"No way." Conn shields the bun from her. "And stop calling me that."

"You suck at sharing."

"*How* unfortunate." He wolfs down the rest of the bun. "At least we don't share a room anymore."

Fin shudders. "Those days will haunt me forever."

"I know how that is." Dawn grunts. "My sister farts around the clock."

"Sounds like someone I know," Conn says behind his hand.

Fin throws a balled-up napkin at him. The three of them laugh.

I pick at my sticky bun. I feel it happening again. My body turning to stone. My throat closing up. The bubble forming, or the membrane, or whatever it is.

There were so many topics they could have picked. Soccer. Spaceships. Siamese cats. If they'd chosen anything else, I could have found something to say. But siblings? I know nothing about them. I'm the only one at this table who doesn't have any. How am I supposed to think of something to say? I should have left when I had the chance. I could have lived without the sticky bun.

Fin, Conn, and Dawn are now debating who's worst off: the youngest, the oldest, or the middle child.

"Definitely the oldest." Dawn points a thumb at her chest.

"I don't know," Conn says. "At our house, the oldest gets the basement to himself. With his own private entrance."

"Really?"

"That's because Dónal's a suck-up." Fin snorts. "Mom and Dad don't see his devil horns."

How long have I been sitting here? Conn glances at me. I know that look. It's the same look Mel gave me at lunch during those first days of school. It was my inconsistency that confused her then. It's my inconsistency that's confusing Conn now. I should have said something right away, as soon as the others sat down. Maybe I still can. Maybe it's not too late.

But the bubble thickens with each passing second—my own personal snow globe. If someone were to pick it up and shake it, all the snow and glitter would move, but not me. I'm the figurine frozen in the midst of it all. I'm starting to think Sakya Pandita got things backward. If the talkative parrot is shut up in a cage—if birds without speech are supposed to be free—then why do I feel like the trapped one right now?

"He can't be as evil as my sister." Dawn flicks her hair.

"Wanna bet?" Fin pulls a dollar out of her pocket.

"Save your money, Dawn." Conn shakes his head. "You'll lose."

The businesswoman stands at the cash register buying something in a cake-sized box. My eyes fall to the doll cake in the display case. Barbie is watching me. I know what she wants to tell me. *Say something. Open your mouth.* But like me, she can't talk. Unlike me, she has a legitimate excuse.

I never thought I'd envy a doll.

Say something. Open your mouth.

But it's too hard. The bubble is too thick, too strong.

Besides, I'm safe here in my bubble. Why should I have to pop it anyway? Why should I have to prove myself to anyone? Why should I have to compete with all the noise? There's freedom of speech, so there should be freedom of no speech. What's that phrase cops use when they're making an arrest? *You have the right to remain silent.*

I have the right to remain silent.

I feel Fin and Dawn looking at me sideways now, an awareness growing. An awareness that it's been ten minutes, and one person at the table hasn't said anything.

Suddenly, the most important thing is to leave, to get out.

As Fin and Dawn go to the counter to order milk shakes, still debating, Conn leans in. "Everything okay?"

I nod, too quickly. "Just tired. Didn't sleep last night." Of course *now* the bubble pops. Go figure.

"Shoot. Wouldn't have kept you if I'd known."

I think he buys my excuse. It's hard to tell. But I know it will only last so long. When I use the same excuse next time, and the time after that, he'll catch on. Luckily, there won't be a next time. It was nice while it lasted. He would have found out about me eventually. The blank slate fills in. The adjective attaches. *Quiet, quiet, quiet.*

I stand.

Conn stands too. "Heading out?"

I nod again.

"All right." His hands find his pockets.

I almost leave without saying anything. But there's a crease in his brow and a heaviness in his slouch, as if he's trying to figure out what he did wrong. I don't like that I made someone look that way.

"My mom needs help with something." The lie tumbles out of me. "It's just us two at home, so…"

Conn's brow relaxes a little. His shoulders too. "Ah, gotcha. Duty calls." He jangles the change in his pocket. "Well, then, guess I'll see you later."

I'm ready to slip past him and get the heck out of here, but he's still looking at me. The girls pause in their argument at the counter, looking too.

"Adios," I squeak. Then I walk—try not to run—out the door.

Adios? I cringe on the curb. *Bye* or *later* would have sufficed. Or no word at all. I hurry down the sidewalk, annoyed because my happiness was disrupted. Annoyed because I can't go to Patsy's Pastries anymore. Annoyed because really, Conn, Fin, and Dawn did nothing wrong. Annoyed because the truth is, even if they hadn't been talking about siblings—even if they'd been talking about soccer or spaceships or Siamese cats—I still wouldn't have said anything.

I take a bite of my half-eaten sticky bun and walk to the bike rack. A man rounds the corner and bumps into me. My last bit of happiness drops to the ground. "Sorry," the man grumbles, hustling past. I watch the bun roll away and almost laugh. The world can't let me eat one little sticky bun in peace. The problem, I decide, is other people. Other people taint everything. They bump into you, try to talk to you, interrupt your happiness, knock it to the ground.

I mount my bike and push off, glancing mournfully at my bun's remains. There's already a bird pecking at them.

Its feathers are black, almost bluish in the setting sun.

The bird looks up at me.

A car beeps. I realize I swerved out of the bike lane. I stop to regain my balance and look back across the street. The bun is there, but the bird isn't.

I push off again, cold creeping through me. I whiz down Main Street and turn toward home. I catch myself scanning the sky and the trees. Ravens are common, aren't they? Like sparrows and squirrels. It couldn't have been the same one.

It couldn't have been Beady.

Now I'm even more annoyed because I'm letting a bird get to me. That's how bad this day—this week—this school year—is going.

CHAPTER 8

THE FRONT DOOR GROANS as I open it. I glare at the hinges and tiptoe up the stairs.

"How was school?"

I wince. So close.

I turn to find my mother in the living room knitting a scarf. "Good." The fib rolls off my tongue.

"You're home late."

"I joined the track team."

"Oh? Good for you." She doesn't look up from her work. I suppose she doesn't want to mess up the stitching. I was hoping to keep avoiding her, in case she asks about her door being open. I just need to get by before she has a chance...

"And how are classes?"

"Fine." I turn toward the hall.

"Everyone being nice?"

My eyes slide back to her. Normally she doesn't ask this many questions. She must be either really bored or gearing up to ask about the door. "Mmm-hmm," I say, hoping that will satisfy her.

"Even that girl?"

"What girl?"

Her knitting needles fly, dip, and weave, scooping up loops of yarn. "You know. The one who commented on your eyebrows."

My jaw locks. Just when I've forgotten about that, she has to swoop in and remind me.

"Remember, she's just jealous." She knits faster. "Anyone who says things like that is jealous."

Is this her attempt to say something motherly? Maybe I should give her credit for trying, but that's the thing: it feels like she's *trying*, forcing it, reciting lines from a script. Like she never got the instincts other mothers have. I didn't notice so much when I was little, but the more time I spent at Mel's, the more I picked up on all the things her mother does that mine doesn't do with me. Like make eye contact. Or kiss me on the forehead when I'm going out the door. Or say things like *sweetheart* and *love you*. Even Miss Looping calls me *honey* sometimes, and she's not anyone's mother. It's not that I need my mother to do these things. It's not that I need her to do anything except, I don't know…interact with me as though it's not an obligation. Maybe then it wouldn't feel like an obligation for me either.

"Right." I start down the hall.

"Oh, could you make sure your window's shut?"

"Uh-huh." I keep walking.

"Don't want more creatures getting in."

I pause. "Creatures?"

"Nothing to worry about. I left my window open yesterday, and a bird flew in."

"A bird?" I look at her over my shoulder.

"Scared the wits out of me." She half laughs. "I ran outside and drove off. And when I got back, I couldn't find it. Must have flown back out."

I squeeze my backpack strap. So that's why her door was open a crack?

"What kind of bird?" I ask in spite of myself.

"Might've been a crow?" She knits a few more stitches and sets down the scarf. "I didn't get a good look. At least it wasn't a bat."

I stare after her as she goes into the kitchen. So I haven't been imagining him. My mother saw him too. The raven was here at the house.

I've heard of people having stalkers, human ones like

that boy who had a crush on Mel last year. Mel told me how he'd follow her around school and wait at her locker and keep asking for her phone number. At least that bordered on flattering. But whoever heard of a *bird* stalker?

And what does he want?

I turn onto my stomach and slide my hands under my pillow to keep them warm. I hate this time of night. This is when things settle, sink in, suspend. This is when events replay. A glance from Mel in the hall. A grade on a project. A boy with binoculars in Patsy's Pastries. His words in my head, echoing. *Hey, Elise.*

I blink in the dark. I wonder if it means anything when someone calls you by name. When they remember your name though they've only met you once. *Hey, Elise.*

It seems…personal.

I can't stop the tingle of warmth that spreads across my scalp, like the one I feel when Mel brushes—used to brush—my hair, and when I read Miss Looping's comments on my papers.

And then the other feeling, that stiffening of muscles, that churning or burning or yearning in my stomach, like the one I felt when I used to sit at Mel's lunch table, and when Fin and Conn and Dawn were joking in the pastry shop.

I want more than anything to fall asleep.

I grab my earbuds and jam them deep in my ears, turn on the music, and raise the volume as high as it will go.

But I still hear words echoing.

Hey, Elise. Hey, Elise.

My throat scratches. I get out of bed and tiptoe down the hall past my mother's closed door. In the kitchen, the digital clock on the microwave says 3:01 a.m. At least I don't have to get up for school in the morning. I open the fridge, its blast of light blinding in the dark. I chug orange juice from the carton. When I finish, I notice the expiration date has passed. My mother never misses something like that. Is she testing me to see if I'll throw it away?

I put the carton back in the fridge and close the door. I sigh and open it again. What's the point in keeping expired juice around just to prove a point? I take the carton over to the sink to dump it out.

Something flashes past the kitchen window.

I put down the orange juice and lean over the sink, looking out and trying to spot my stalker.

A weak glow in the shed's window draws my eyes.

Expired orange juice gurgles in my stomach. And something comes back to me. A figure in the night, out there by the shed. I thought it had been a trick of the light or the unsleep. Had I seen someone?

The light flickers. Movement.

I duck to the floor as thoughts fly through my head, each crazier than the one before: A fugitive is camping out in there, hiding from the law. Or a serial killer, planning an attack. Or a werewolf, lying low until a full moon.

Before my thoughts can spiral further, I crawl across the kitchen floor. Once I reach the hall, I get to my feet and hurry to my mother's door. For the first time since I was maybe five, I knock.

No answer. I knock again. Is she ignoring me? I knock a third time. My heart bangs in my chest. What if the trespasser outside can hear me knocking? I twist the knob. It's not locked. I push the door open. I don't care if it's the middle of the night; I don't care if she doesn't want me going in her room. This is an emergency. We need to call the police.

I flip on the light and stare at my mother's bed: empty, unmade, the covers flung down.

I watch the shed through the gap in my curtains, not daring to part them more than an inch.

The patch of light in the window blinks out. I suck in my breath.

The moonlight catches on a shape coming out of the shed door: a slight hunch, wisps of hair, the bulk of a nightgown.

The orange juice swishes again in my stomach. I watch my mother's silvery outline close the door, lingering a moment. Then she turns back toward the house, disappearing into shadow.

I jump onto my bed and lie flat on my back, listening.

A minute later, there's a creak in the hall. The slightest click of her bedroom door. The back entrance to the house is a sliding door, so it doesn't groan like the front door, and I'm sure it wouldn't make a sound if someone slid it very, very slowly, which is no doubt what my mother just did. That explains why I didn't hear her come in last time either.

I lie this way for a while, waiting.

The silence continues.

I climb out of bed and change into jeans, a jacket, and sneakers. Grabbing a flashlight from my closet, I tiptoe to the back door. I slide it open the way my mother would have— very, very slowly—and trek through the overgrowth toward the shed. The woods push against the fence, as if they're leaning to see who goes there. I shiver but keep walking.

When I reach the shed, I shine the flashlight in the little side window, illuminating the filth on the glass and the rusty shovels and rakes leaning against it, blocking whatever lies beyond it. More of the same, I always assumed. But what would my mother want with past residents' yard tools in the middle of the night?

I go around to the shed door and shine the light on the latch. I try to slide the bolt, but the rust on the metal causes so much friction that I have to jerk it little by little until, without warning, it jerks all the way out and scrapes my knuckles against the wood of the door.

I rub my hands and wipe the rust off, staring at the door. I take a step back. What if there are dead bodies in there? Or a secret laboratory, or—

No. I didn't get dressed and come all the way out here and scrape my knuckles just to chicken out. Just to go back to bed and lie wide awake wondering. Even if I might not like what I'll find, I'd rather know.

I breathe in and push open the door.

The beam of my flashlight reveals small cardboard boxes and a battery-powered lantern. I turn the lantern on. It flickers once before shedding a dim glow—the glow I must have seen from my bedroom window. I look around. Other than the rakes and shovels leaning against the window, there are just half a dozen boxes. That's it. Not that I *wanted* to find dead bodies or a secret laboratory…but I can't help feeling underwhelmed. Then again, when has my mother ever been interesting?

I move to the nearest box and lift the flaps. A pacifier, baby shoes, a checkered bib. I pull out a worn envelope packed with photographs. In the first picture, a baby crawls on a carpet, smiling, reaching toward the camera, with big eyebrows and a curlicue of dark hair. I stare. Is that me? I didn't think my mother had any pictures of me.

I leaf through more. Another of the baby, this time in a sandbox.

Then there are two in the sandbox, one a baby, the other a toddler.

Then they're at a playground together. Then they're on Santa's lap. Then they're squinting in front of some church, dressed in little suits and ties.

Boys. They're both boys, with eyebrows that almost meet in the middle.

In another picture, the boys sit on a park bench. The older boy is blowing bubbles through a bubble wand. The smaller boy hugs a teddy bear wearing a bow tie. He looks like he's about to cry.

I turn the picture over. Someone has jotted in slanting letters: *Eustace age 2, Emerson age 4.* The handwriting looks like my mother's.

In the next photograph, the boys aren't alone. The two of them stand on either side of a dark-haired pregnant woman. Behind them, a tall mustached man grins over their heads, raising a beer bottle to the camera. The woman beams down at the boys as they lean in kissing her baby bump. She's slimmer than my mother—except for the belly—and younger. But her face is unmistakable.

If I were to guess what my mother looked like ten or fifteen years ago, this would be it.

I turn the picture over, and for once there's a date: seven days before I was born. And a caption in that same slanting hand, with a smiley face drawn next to it: *E & E kissing their sis.*

I drop the photograph on the floor as if it seared my fingers. The caption stares back at me. That word, *sis.* I push the first box aside, finding other boxes behind it, labeled with names in black marker. *Emerson*, one says. *Eustace*, says another. I pull open the flaps of a box labeled *Emerson*. Inside there's a heap of stuff: Hot Wheels. Building blocks. A fraying Batman blanket. I move to a box labeled *Eustace*. A rubber ducky. A picture book about a tap-dancing turtle. A teddy bear wearing a bow tie—just like the one in the photograph.

My chest tightens as I run my fingers over the bear's fur, the worn spots, the places where someone squeezed him too many times.

"Don't touch that."

I jump and look up. My mother stands in the shed's doorway, her knuckles white.

CHAPTER 9

I T'S ODD SEEING HER in her nightgown. In the mornings, she's already dressed when I leave for school. After dinner, we go to our rooms and shut our doors. But seeing her out here in the middle of the night, her graying hair a mess, purple bags underscoring her eyes, makes me think I have two mothers I don't know instead of one. She's only a few feet from me, but she seems farther, like at the movies when you see and hear the actors, but if you were to try to touch them, all you'd feel is the movie screen.

"Put it back." My mother's glower fixes on the teddy bear. "You shouldn't be in here."

Her words barely reach me through the fog in my head. "What is all this?" I blink at the teddy bear, at the other toys, at the pictures fanned out on the floor. "Whose stuff is this?"

My mother makes a show of rubbing her eyes. "I'm too tired for this right now. Just go to your room." She steps inside, away from the doorway, so I can get by.

I stay where I am and hold up the photograph of the boys kissing the pregnant woman's belly. It shakes because my hand shakes. "Who are these people?"

She glances at the photograph. Her fingers twitch at her sides, as if itching for something to knit, for an excuse to not meet my eyes.

"Is this you?" I point to the pregnant woman in the photograph.

"I said go to your room."

"Is it?"

She doesn't say no. Why doesn't she just say no?

Something about the lighting in here dizzies me. It was all a trick—the high grass around the shed, and the tools at the window, rusting like the door latch... They were all meant to add to the illusion, to make me believe there was nothing but rubble and spiderwebs in here.

I push away the photograph. "This is messed up."

"Excuse me?"

I gesture at the boxes, the toys, the pictures. "This is all crazy." My words rush out in a croak-laugh. "Some crazy joke."

"You think I'm crazy?" There's that flash in her eyes, one I've seen before.

I don't move. I half expect her to grab me, to drag me

from the shed, to throw me over the fence and into the woods. To discard me like she's always wanted to. This is her chance. I brace myself.

"You shouldn't have said that," she hisses through her teeth. "You shouldn't say things when you don't even know what you're talking about. You have no idea what I've been through with your brothers and—" She presses her lips together.

"Brothers?" I stiffen.

She winces and closes her eyes.

"I don't have any brothers." My words sound far off, as if someone is talking outside.

"Are you happy now?" she murmurs. "You wanted to know who it all belongs to."

"I don't have any brothers."

Her eyes open, shiny now, and find mine through the movie screen. "You think I haven't wanted to tell you? If you'd had the decency not to snoop around, you would have found out the right way. At the right time..." She balls up her fists and looks around at all the boxes. Her eyes seem to strain, as if seeing other things. "Go ahead, call me a bad mother. Everyone else did. No one understood why I couldn't keep them here. No one except..." A sound erupts somewhere in her throat, an ugly gurgle. Then she's turning, running through the doorway and across the backyard, disappearing around the side of the house.

I clutch my stomach, listening. I hear the station wagon start and the wheels roll off down the gravel, down the hill, into the night—or more like the morning.

No one understood why I couldn't keep them here. What did she mean?

I turn and tear through the rest of the boxes. An Etch A Sketch, a Mr. Potato Head, a kaleidoscope. More toys that weren't mine. Used coloring books, stationery, cards. No birthday cards this time, but cards with phrases like *Thinking of You* or *With Sympathy* on the front. I glance inside some of them. Vague notes addressed to my mother have been scribbled to personalize printed verses.

Deepest sympathies and healing prayers.
Very sorry to hear about the accident.
Devastated to learn what happened yesterday.

I linger on the last card's date: April 14th. I was born on the thirteenth.

Sweat spreads across my forehead and the back of my neck. I force myself to look inside the other cards.

Hang in there, hon. God's testing your faith.
To think they were minutes from
you and the baby... I'm so sorry.
Condolences for your loss — praying your sons will pull through.

I sit back on my haunches. *The accident...your loss...*
I knew a drunk driver had killed my father when I was a
baby. My mother had told me that much. But I didn't know it
had happened the day I was born. A feeling overwhelms me,
bulging in the center of my gut: It happened because of me.
My father was driving to see *me* at the hospital or wherever I
was. And it sounds like he wasn't alone in the car. The sweat
on my neck trickles down my back.

The boys... What became of the boys? My...brothers?

The phrase rings strange in my head. *My brothers*. Did
they "pull through"?

I dig for more cards, more clues. I search every box in
the room again, throwing contents over my shoulder. But I
find nothing else, nothing to answer the rest of my questions,
to settle the dread and orange juice squirming in my belly.

And my mother has left me here by myself.

I try to think through the fog of the unsleep. She said
belongs. The stuff *belongs* to my brothers. Present tense, not

past. She wouldn't have said that if they hadn't "pulled through," would she?

I push away the papers and close my eyes. My head hurts from straining to make sense of things. What I wouldn't give, suddenly, for it to be yesterday, when all I had to worry about was my tally and where to go during lunch. What I wouldn't give to be in the cafeteria contemplating how to avoid one of Sylvia's open-ended questions.

At some point, seconds or minutes later, something clamors behind me. I jump and turn. One of the rakes is on the floor; it must have slipped. The sound rouses my muscles back to life, pushing me out the door, into the house, and up the stairs to my bedroom. I dump schoolbooks and papers out of my backpack and repack it with things within reach—socks, jeans, T-shirts, a sweatshirt. I pick up my notebook, the one with my tallies, and finger its worn edges, its familiar spirals. I slip it in my bag too, and then force a comb through my tangles before sticking in barrettes to keep my hair out of my face. I haven't slept in ages, but my thoughts couldn't be clearer. I know what I have to do. I lift my pillow and grab the birthday card from Granny P, eyeing the return address in the top left corner of the envelope—the zip code that's two numbers off from mine. If my mother won't tell me anything, I'll get answers from someone else.

I slip the card in my backpack. Then I pass through the kitchen, filling a thermos with water and grabbing a box of crackers before heading out the front door.

For the first time in seven months, I'm on Mel's front steps. I'm not sure what time it is. The air is cool, but the sun is up, and I can hear the clang of pots and pans from the kitchen window. I lean my bike against the railing and ring the doorbell. My knees shake. I tell myself it's because of the bike ride.

As I wait, a shape hovers in the corner of my eye—something sitting on the fencepost. I turn in time to see a jet-black bird flying away, but right now I don't have the energy to care.

Mrs. Asimakos answers the door in her bathrobe. "Oh. Elise." She smiles. "Haven't seen you in a while."

Somehow I manage to smile back.

"We've missed you around here. Would you like some pancakes? I'm about to make a batch."

"No, thank you. I...was wondering if I could print

something." I was always able to talk to Mrs. Asimakos, at least here at the house. But it's been seven months since I've spoken to her, so my words come out a little wobbly. Or maybe that's the unsleep.

"Of course. Come on in."

I step into the foyer. It still smells of pinewood. I look around at the familiar relics: the coatrack, the umbrella stand, the shoe mat. The half-moon table with framed pictures of Mel and her sister. Beyond that is the doorway to the living room, where Mel and I used to tinker with her father's old camcorder and make "movies," which weren't really movies but bad attempts to keep our faces straight while reciting soap-opera lines we'd made up seconds earlier. We always made a fuss of watching each video after.

"Ew, I look like a fish!" Mel would squeal and cover her eyes.

"Ew, my arms are so awkward!" I'd chime in.

Then we'd reassure each other that no one looked fishy or awkward, and we'd keel over laughing at everything our screen personas said and did. Each "movie" was a blooper reel more than anything else.

It's funny to think of those videos now. If I were to watch one, would I recognize the person next to Mel? I think

I would envy her, a girl who still thinks she can be a movie star. A girl who's still friends with Mel. A girl who hasn't gone to Green Pasture yet. Or started a tally yet.

Or seen what's in the shed yet.

Mrs. Asimakos leads me to the computer in the study room. "I'll go see if Mel's up."

"Thanks."

I sit in the desk chair and pull out the envelope with Granny P's return address. Glen Forest Cottage, North Commons, Scavendish. No street number—that's odd. Maybe she lives in some kind of retirement community. That is, if she still lives there. I look at the card again. *I heard somebody's turning four…* She sent this when I was four, close to nine years ago. I chew the inside of my cheek. A lot can change in nine years. She could have moved. She could be anywhere in the country, the world. I don't even know her real name. She wrote *Granny P* on the envelope and the card. And if somehow she still lives at this address, who's to say she'll know or remember anything about my brothers? Who's to say she's still "with it"? She must be pretty old by now.

She might not even be alive anymore.

But I have to at least try. As long as there's a chance, even a slim one, I have to give it a go.

I type the return address into the computer and look up directions. Google locates North Commons, but not the cottage itself. It's thirty-five minutes north by car. Two hours by bike. Five and a half hours by foot. I click Print.

As the printer whirs, I close my eyes and breathe in. The comfort of Mel's house makes me want to curl up on the soft, clean carpet and let the Asimakoses' cats sniff me all over. I restrain myself. I probably shouldn't be here in the first place. I could have printed directions somewhere else— tried the town library when it opens. But if I could just talk to Mel, tell her about the boxes, the photos, the run-in with my mother, the sympathy cards...she'll overlook my inconsistency this time. I know she's still my friend. I know she'll help me. She'll know what to do, or at least what to say.

Maybe she'll even come with me.

Voices rumble from the kitchen. I grab the directions and move toward the voices and the smell of pancakes.

"Why's she here? It's seven thirty in the morning. On a Saturday."

"She said she needs to print something."

"Well, tell her I'm not home."

I pause halfway down the hall.

"I already told her you're here."

"Tell her I'm sick then."

"Mel, honey, what's going on with you two?"

"Nothing. She's just…gotten weird since school started."

"Weird how?"

"I don't know. She acts rude, like no one's good enough to talk to. Even me. Tell her I'm sick, okay?"

I hear a sigh and footsteps. I back away down the hall. In seconds I'm out the door, mounting my bike, pedaling back up the hill. I don't look back.

Something tells me I'll never pass through that door again.

At my house, my mother's station wagon is still missing from the driveway. I drop my bike in the grass and walk across the backyard without looking at the shed. It will be better to climb the fence and cut through the woods than to use roads. For one thing, I'm less likely to be seen. I don't need people asking where I'm going or telling my mother they saw me. For another, it's more direct. According to the map printout, North Commons sits at the opposite edge of the forest, where a long lane runs up from a road to the green part on the map. The cottage must be off the beaten path. Rather than making an enormous U around the forest, I'll walk straight across, following the stream that runs through the middle—or whatever that blue line on the map is—until I get to the other side. There's no way I can miss it.

As I climb the fence and slip into the woods behind the house, the world looks smudgy like it could be a dream— with the unsleep it's hard to tell—but the drumming of my heart sounds real.

CHAPTER 10

I DON'T FOLLOW A PATH because there isn't one.

I walk straight ahead through the trees, not thinking about anything except how fast I'm moving or how evenly I'm breathing. It's easy to not think about big things when there are so many little things to distract me, like squirrels darting up tree trunks. Sunshine peeking through leaves. Sparrows bursting out of treetops. And then there are the sounds: the squirrels chittering at each other, the leaves whispering in the breeze, the sparrows trilling on their branches.

The woods are having conversations all around me, but no one's expecting me to "participate." And no one's calling me "quiet" when I don't. I could walk forever in these woods. Live here, even. Maybe that makes me weird. Mel called me so, after all. *She's just...gotten weird since school started.*

It's not like I *want* to be weird. It's not like I haven't tried to find a compromise, a work-around, a way to participate from inside the bubble. I thought I'd found one once, that second

Saturday of the school year when I discovered social media. The internet was still new to me then, since my mother didn't let me use it at home. But I'd gotten doses at Mel's house, and that afternoon I biked to the town library and logged on to a computer. Each patron was allowed two hours at a time. Mel had emailed me a link to a website that lots of Green Pasture kids use. You're supposed to be thirteen or older to create an account, but apparently everyone lies about their age, so I did too. I'd be thirteen in less than a year anyway. For my profile picture, I used a photo of Mel and me laughing in her backyard last summer.

I found Mel's account—her picture was a "selfie," as people called it—and browsed her list of "friends." Some names and faces I recognized from class or the halls of Green Pasture, and others I didn't. I went down the list and clicked the Add Friend button next to all eighty-one of them. Clicking was easy. I clicked here; I clicked there. As I waited for everyone to accept my friend requests, I opened the site's instant messaging service and started sending messages. Hi, I said to a girl named Jackie Pincer. Howdy, to some boy named Cody Moretti. Hey, to a bunch of others.

The person in the first chat box responded: Do I know you?

I hesitated and then brought my fingers to the keyboard. No. Well, maybe. I go to Green Pasture. Typing was almost as easy as clicking. I could take as long as I wanted to compose my thoughts and choose my words.

K.

What's up? I typed.

This is weird. Why'd you message me?

Sorry, just trying this thing out.

I don't even know you.

Do you like poetry?

Ummm, not really.

Who's your favorite poet?

I waited for a response. Jackie Pincer didn't reply.

I saw that someone else had responded in another chat box: Who's this?

I typed back. Elise. What's up?

I messaged dozens of people that afternoon, starting conversations like the one with Jackie Pincer. There at my fingertips was a new way of socializing that didn't require me to speak a single word out loud. It was superior even to sign language, because no one could see me or my eyebrows or any food in my teeth. I could be everything online that I wasn't in person. I could be popular at Green Pasture after all.

Monday morning, everyone stared at me in the halls and snickered and whispered.

That's her. She messaged practically everyone in the school.

Sylvia came up to me, followed by Mel and the other girls. "We heard you chatted up a storm this weekend."

"Did you really message all those people?" Mel frowned at me. "People you don't even know?"

It didn't take me long to realize my mistake. I deleted my account that afternoon, but the damage was done.

I look at the sky through the treetops now. It may be true that there's no work-around back home, but here in the woods I don't need one. And when I get to Glen Forest Cottage, maybe I won't need one there either. Maybe Granny P will let me stay with her, and the bubble won't ever come back, and I'll never have to return to school. Sakya Pandita didn't get it backward after all. He just forgot to specify that other birds fly free as long as they're not at school.

I come to a stream that snakes through the trees—the blue line on the map. The water shimmers and winks at me. Only one thing matters now: finding Granny P. Finding out what happened. That's all I need to focus on. I let the stream lead the way.

I catch my eyelids drooping as I walk. I can always count on the unsleep to ease up while I'm in class or doing homework or traveling somewhere important, like right now. Never at night when I'm in bed. That would be too convenient. I jerk my eyes open and pop a piece of gum in my mouth. *Chew, walk, chew, walk.*

Between the smacks of my gum I hear a noise—not squirrels or birds or the leaves in the wind, but a dog barking somewhere.

Somewhere close.

I turn around in time to see a brown shape making a beeline for me through the trees.

My body is slow to react. Somehow my brain gets the message to my legs, and I break into a sprint. My shoelaces flail, but there's no time to fix them. I can hear the dog's collar jangling and a growl edging his bark. I try to imagine I'm at track practice or in my first race, but my legs can't go any faster. Snot clogs my nostrils, and I gulp at the air, pumping my legs, waiting for the dog's fangs to pierce my ankles.

My best bet is to climb a tree, but all the branches look too high. What if I stop and try to climb but can't reach, and then I'm dog food? What will it feel like to be chewed to pieces? I feel water on my cheeks. I must be crying. Behind the barking, I hear something else. Voices? Through the trees I glimpse figures moving, walking.

I never thought I'd be glad to see other people.

"Help!" I yell. Only it comes out as a squeak. But maybe they've heard it because they're coming toward me now. Walking—not running, just strolling, taking their time. Three tall figures, two boys and a girl, all wearing camouflage jackets and hunting boots, with shotguns slung over their shoulders. They look like they could be seventeen or eighteen, older than any kids I know.

"Here, boy." The pigtailed girl whistles and claps, holding out some sort of treat. The hound comes running to her.

I almost keel over, trying to catch my breath. My knees shake. I lean on my thighs and eye the hound, who sniffs at a treat in the girl's hand. He seems to have forgotten about me—for now. But I wish they'd put him on a leash or something.

"Go get it, boy." The girl hurls the treat away like a boomerang. The dog chases it, disappearing among the tree trunks.

The tallest boy, the one with a buzz cut, is looking at me. "Don't worry, her pup's harmless."

I'm not convinced.

He whispers something to his companions, who nod and point at my bag. I adjust my backpack on my shoulders and continue on my way.

"Hey, where are you off to?"

"Don't leave. We're nice."

"Yeah, we're saints."

The three of them snicker.

I pick up my pace.

They come up behind me, the buzz-cut boy on my left and the other two on my right.

"Aren't you going to say thank you? We did just save your life, didn't we?"

I look straight ahead and keep walking. If I ignore them, they'll get bored. That tactic always works at Green Pasture. When I don't make a sound, people eventually lose interest. Even Sylvia with all her questions. To keep someone's interest, you have to say things.

The buzz-cut boy steps in front of me. "I asked you a question."

I try to walk around him, but he steps the same way.

"Maybe she doesn't know English," says the shorter boy with the curly hair.

The girl grunts. "She said 'help,' doofus."

The buzz-cut boy nods at my backpack. "Whatcha got in there? Any tokens of your appreciation?"

More snickers.

I skirt around him.

He blocks my path again. "Let's have a look."

As I pivot to walk past him, he wrenches my backpack off my arms. I try to grab it from him, but he scoots back and holds the bag above my head, dangling it out of my reach. I jump for it. The other two cackle. He tosses it to the curly-haired boy, who tosses it to the girl, who tosses it back to the buzz-cut boy, all while I spin around trying to snatch it. Heat engulfs my face. The buzz-cut boy unzips my backpack. I lunge for it, but he jumps back and holds it up again, laughing. "Hold her off, will you?" he says. "She doesn't want to make this easy."

The girl and the curly-haired boy yank my wrists behind me and push me to the ground, pinning me there on my stomach. I jerk and squirm and try to shake them off, swallowing my gum and some dirt in the process. They put their weight on me with their hands and elbows, and one of them rests the sole of a boot against my cheek, pressing my face into the ground. I can't move my head or see the buzz-cut boy behind me, but I can hear him rifling through my backpack.

"Anything good?" says the girl.

"Crackers. Gum." Another pocket unzips. "A library card. A pen…"

The more I wriggle, the tighter the two accomplices grip my wrists. The harder the boot pushes on my face.

"Aha. Jackpot."

The girl snorts. "A birthday card?"

"Look what's inside."

I don't need to see it to know what he's found. The hundred-dollar bill. The money for my college fund.

His companions whoop in unison.

I hate them, but not as much as I hate myself for letting them be stronger than me. If only I had gotten more sleep, saved more strength... Or would it make any difference? They're older, bigger, and carrying shotguns. They could hold me at gunpoint if they wanted to. Even if I were stronger, I wouldn't be able to fight off bullets.

"We're rich," crows the curly-haired boy above me.

"*We're?*" I hear the buzz-cut boy cluck his tongue. "Sorry, finders keepers."

"What?" The girl's grip on my wrists loosens. "We split it *three* ways. That's only fair."

"Okay, fine, three ways. Mark, you can have the library card. Dakota, you get the pen. And I get the hundred."

The curly-haired boy's grip slackens now too. "You're kidding, right?"

My head pounds as they argue over my money. I close my eyes, wishing I could fade into darkness. What will happen to me if I just lie here? Will they go away? Will they kill me?

Kraaa.

A deep croak. A beating of wings above me.

My eyelids weigh a hundred pounds each, but I manage to blink them open. All I see is dirt.

Kraaa.

The croaking rises. Wings beat harder. Is that who I think it is? I wriggle and squirm, trying to pull my cheek out from under the boot to see what's going on.

"What in the…"

"Ouch!"

I twist with all my might. I still can't move my head, so I throw up my ankles, jamming them into someone's leg. The hands that bind me hesitate, loosening even more.

Kraaa.

I hear all three hunters shouting over the croaking. In one motion, I rip my wrists free and jerk my right elbow back, shoving it into another leg. There's a yelp—the curly-haired boy, I think—and the boot's pressure lifts from my cheek. I slam my other elbow into someone's thigh, and then

I glimpse the girl's boots as she stumbles backward into the buzz-cut boy. I jump to my feet and run.

Crack-boom.

A gunshot. I cover my head but keep running. I'm still alive, still breathing. And the *kraaa*s haven't stopped yet. I'm tempted to look back to see if it's him...my stalker. Was he helping me?

But I can't afford to do anything that might slow my momentum, so I keep my eyes ahead and fly on through the trees as the commotion fades behind me. The faster I run, the sooner I'll reach the finish line. But where is the finish line? I've been running away from the stream, I realize, and my backpack is back there with the directions. The map.

But I can't go back now. If I want to stay alive, I can only keep running.

CHAPTER 11

RAIN POKES MY FACE, light at first, and then faster and heavier. I dare to glance over my shoulder: nothing but trees. I listen: no gunshots, no footsteps, no barking either. I've done it—I've lost the hunters. Or, more likely, they didn't think me worth the trouble of chasing. I've lost the stream too, but it can't be far. I fight the numbness in my legs and pull up my hood, wishing I'd worn something waterproof. Why didn't I check the weather forecast before I left? Why did I leave in the first place?

Clearly, it was a mistake. Just like opening my mouth is a mistake, every time. Yelling out to those hunters cost me my backpack and everything in it. Calling my mother crazy made her run off, when maybe if I'd kept my words inside, she would have explained things, and I wouldn't be out here lost and wet and shaking. But with my mouth closed there's no winning either: I'm "quiet." I'm weird. It's a vicious circle, just like these woods seem to be.

The rain pounds against my hood. I spot a hollow at the base of a tree and duck into it, pulling my knees toward me. I close my eyes because a headache is digging its way across my forehead, and I have no clue where I am, and my teeth won't stop chattering.

I don't know how long it takes for the rain to stop, but all of a sudden I can't hear it anymore. The hush startles me. I pull myself out of the hollow and brush myself off. I like things quiet, but this is too quiet. What happened to all the conversations? All the squirrels and chipmunks and birds— the little distractions? The rain must have driven them into their burrows and nests.

I find myself growing jumpy, spooking when water drips from a leaf onto my head, spying shadows in the corners of my eyes. When I turn, nothing is there. I've heard stories of travelers alone in the wilderness losing their minds. Going insane. But I didn't think it could happen this quickly. I've only been gone a matter of hours. How many hours? I wish I'd remembered my watch.

A flash of black stirs the trees, another shadow that comes to nothing. I have no idea if I'm going the right way. I can't remember the directions, can't picture the map. But a person can't go far these days without bumping into buildings, houses, civilization. The trees will have to start thinning soon. Another town will have to emerge. When I get there, the first thing I'll do is find a coffee shop or a convenience store and dry off. After that, I'll force myself, somehow, to ask someone for directions to North Commons.

But what if it gets to be sunset and I still haven't found my way out?

Don't panic. Focus. Don't panic.

My head throbs. I wish I had some aspirin.

There it is again—a flash of black in the trees. And there. My eyes dart around in spite of myself, trying to pin down the source.

There. Then in that tree there. Now that one.

Little eyes looking at me.

To my surprise, relief washes over me. The hunters didn't get him.

He zips to another tree.

I chase him, tripping over roots. He whizzes in and out of trees, keeping just out of sight. My relief gives way to frustration, fueling me even in my exhaustion. I open my mouth to call after him. *Hey, you! I know you're there!* Then I realize how ridiculous that would be: me talking to a bird. Not to mention dangerous. The hunters might hear me and track me down.

I shut my mouth and stumble after the raven, trying to spot him among the leaves, but I've already lost him.

I slow to a trudge, letting my feet drag through the mud. All I see are trees now, and all I hear are my footsteps. And a buzzing in my ears, harsh against the silence. The hollowness in my ears grows hollower. The buzzing louder.

Then something tickles my eardrums. I perk up. There, behind the buzzing, I hear it. A floating tune. Music. Or maybe the silence has folded in on itself and it's not really music I'm hearing, but some auditory illusion.

I follow the sound anyway.

It's easy to follow when it's the only sound there is. It's so precious that my ears cling to it as it leads me farther and farther on. I don't have much energy left, but I manage to jog. First I think it's coming from this tree. Then that tree. Then that tree over there.

Then just like that, the trees stop and the earth drops. I halt before I drop with it, and I find myself standing on a mossy ledge. It plunges toward rocks and brambles. A wave of vertigo floods me. I step back and put my hand out to steady myself on a tree, but I find it's better if I just sit down. I close my eyes. After a moment, the dizziness fades enough that I can take in the view before me: a yellow one-story house no taller than the cliff I'm on. Trees hem in all sides of the clearing except my side, where the cliff closes it off from the rest of the forest, zigzagging to my left and my right and disappearing back into the trees. I doubt that anyone would notice this house unless they sat where I'm sitting.

The music is closer than ever.

Something moves on the front porch of the house. I crouch behind a tree trunk and squint. Someone is sitting there, I realize, half hidden by a post, playing a violin: a boy, maybe a few years older than me. He must have been playing there the whole time.

The front door of the house opens. A woman with a braid of white hair steps onto the porch and puts a tea tray on a table. The boy stops playing and sets the violin on his lap. As he moves toward the table, I see he's using his arms to roll himself in a wheelchair. The old woman pours three cups of tea and sits in a rocking chair, just as another boy in a wheelchair glides out and joins them. They all sip their tea and gesture with their hands. I can't understand what they're saying, but I hear laughter. Not like the cackling of the buzz-cut boy's cohort, but a light laughter that reminds me of wind chimes. Then the second boy picks up a case off the floor and opens it, taking out another violin.

Both boys raise their instruments and nod.

A fast-paced jig sends currents of life through my veins. These aren't violins I'm hearing now, but fiddles—a different kind of music born from the same strings. The old woman claps along. The boys bob their heads as they slide the bows back and forth. They're far enough away that I can't discern the details of their faces, only square jaws and thick eyebrows. So thick that I can see, even from here, how they almost meet in the middle.

My heart beats with the old woman's clapping and then surpasses it, racing. It's too easy. And yet, isn't it them? The boys from the photographs, but taller, older? And the wheelchairs... Did a car accident put them in those wheelchairs?

This must be Glen Forest Cottage. Granny P's place. Of course. They've been living with Granny P this whole time!

As I listen, I already know that as soon as they see me, everything will be fine—more than fine. I'm not even worried about what to say or do. I can barely stop myself from springing to my feet and flailing my arms and shouting across the clearing.

But I want to do this right. I *have* to do this right. I've come too far not to.

I notice some wildflowers growing near my feet, yellow like the cottage. I smile. There are three. It's meant to be. I'll give one flower to each of them, and then I'll explain who I am, but they'll know it's me anyway when they see my eyebrows, and we'll cry and laugh and kiss and hug. Maybe my brothers will tease me for giving such a girlie gift. "Flowers...that's something only our sis would do." And they'll tousle my hair, kind of like I saw Conn do to Fin once, and they'll hug me again, and they'll play me a jig, and maybe I'll clap, even dance, and then I'll bring them home, Granny P too, and my mother will be able to look at me and will maybe even bake a cake that we'll all share on my birthday, and every year will go on that way. I see exactly how it could be.

The problem is getting to the cottage. This cliff is high enough that I can't jump it.

As the boys finish their jig and start another, I spot a path coming out of the woods at the right side of the cottage. There—I need to find that path. That should be easy since I haven't seen any other paths around; it must be the only one. I pull the flowers out of the ground: one, two, three. Stealing one more glance at the merriment on the porch, I veer right and follow the cliff edge. My whole body trembles with excitement. Who will catch sight of me first? Will it be Emerson? Eustace? Granny P? Maybe all three will turn and see me at once.

I hurry along, waiting for the ground to slope down and

the cliff edge to end. It keeps going. It has already taken me so far that, when I look back, I can't see the glen anymore—only trees. I peer down at more trees below. Still too high to jump. I run faster along the edge, squeezing the flowers' stems. The light through the trees weakens, and the wind picks up, whipping and nipping me. Then, finally, the ground slopes down, down, down, until the woods become level once more. I veer to the left, back in the direction of the glen, irked at how far the cliff took me. But it's okay—I just have to find the path.

Where is the path?

Time slips, and precious daylight with it. The path doesn't show itself.

Did I pass it? Did I go too far to the left? Or not far enough? I turn in place, round and round. It's here somewhere. I just need to concentrate. I realize I can't hear the music anymore. My ears strain against the wind. Maybe my brothers stopped playing. Maybe they went inside the cottage. They must have.

Or am I farther away than I thought?

More trees. No path.

I try the opposite direction. More trees. No path.

I circle this way, then that, listening for the music, watching for the path, waiting for the woods to open up, for the cottage to appear out of the trees, welcoming me.

It doesn't.

How could I have lost it so fast? Sweat seeps through my clothes despite the cold. I turn back, trying to retrace my steps as I fight against the wind.

But when enough time has passed that I should be back where I started, I'm not. And the woods are dimming. My vision is dimming. If I could just think straight, figure out where I took a wrong turn...

Something like vertigo floods me again, only I'm nowhere near a cliff this time. I slump to my knees, dropping the flowers. It isn't fair. The cottage was right in front of my eyes. My brothers were right in front of my eyes. I dig my fingers into the ground, letting dirt clump under my nails. Tears sting my cheeks.

The raven lands on the ground near me. He's probably come to mock me with his stare, but I don't have the strength to care. I let him watch as I lie down on my side. Pine needles press lines into my cheek, and acorns prod my ribs. More teardrops dribble off my face because holding them in takes too much effort.

"Don't cry, love."

I blink. Through the tears I see an old woman standing in the shadow of a tree. The Beady look-alike swoops up onto her shoulder.

I sit up slowly and squint. As leafy shadows flicker over her, I catch hints of a nose, a chin, a white braid flapping in the wind. Though it's hard to make her out, I feel sure of one thing: she's the woman I saw at the cottage with my brothers.

"Are you my grandmother?" I wipe my cheeks.

"Look at you..." The old woman's—Granny P's?—voice is a wheeze, a whisper I can hardly hear over the wind. "Spitting image of the boys."

The boys. My brothers. "Can I meet them?" My voice cracks.

The old woman hesitates. The shadows keep dancing over her, and I wish they'd stop so I could get a good look at her.

"Don't they want to meet me?" I wring my hands. I should have known. I'm the reason they're in wheelchairs after all. Why would they want anything to do with me?

"Of course they do." Granny P's shape starts to shrink, backing away. "But it's not the right time. The truth is you shouldn't be here, and I shouldn't—" A gust of wind in my ear cuts her off. Her shape turns, disappearing behind a tree trunk.

"Wait." I fumble to my feet, calling after her. "Wait. Why are my brothers here? Why did my mother send them away?" No answer. I run to the tree trunk and peer behind it. Just shadows. I listen for her voice in the wind and search for her figure in the fading light, finding neither. How could she leave me already? After I came all this way?

"You'll understand soon."

I whirl around.

The old woman stands in the shadow of a different tree, the raven still on her shoulder, preening his feathers.

"Does that mean I'll get to see them?" Hope rises in my chest.

"Just wait until your birthday, love."

"My birthday?"

"That was the agreement."

I remember something my mother said in the shed... *You would have found out the right way. At the right time...* Did she mean my thirteenth birthday?

"You'll get your birthday present this year." Granny P darkens each time I blink. She's almost as dark as the raven now. "As long as—" Another blast of wind clouts my ears.

"As long as what?"

"Don't say a word to anyone," I hear. "Can you do that for me? For the boys?"

The raven stops preening, as if waiting for my answer.

Leaves waltz around me, tickling my face, blowing through my hair, drying my tears. "Yes." I've never felt so sure of anything. "But are my brothers okay?"

"Don't worry about them." The old woman nods, and the raven takes off, soaring up above me. "They're well looked after."

A calmness settles over me. I tilt my head skyward and watch the raven fly through the treetops, out of sight. As the wind dies, I draw my eyes back to Granny P. But she isn't there. Leaves and feathers flutter to the ground. I search behind tree trunks and swivel my head in all directions, but it's no use: I'm alone.

CHAPTER 12

*D*ON'T SAY A WORD *to anyone.*

I pluck a black feather off the ground and stare at it. Between my fingers, it dances in and out of focus. I try to concentrate. Did Granny P mean any word at all? Or only words about my brothers? I probably should have asked. But she came and went so quickly, so quietly. It makes me wonder what sort of person could do that, what sort of old woman would live out here in the woods. What sort of lady a raven would perch on. Someone different, someone witchy... Not bad-witchy, though. She was good-witchy—I could tell. And maybe if she trusts the raven, I should too. Is that why he's been stalking me? Because Granny P sent him to look after me?

It takes a lot of effort to raise my arm, but I manage to clip the feather in my hair with one of my barrettes. If Granny P meant only certain words, she would have said so. And even if she did mean certain words, knowing me, I'd let those words slip, say something I shouldn't, something about my brothers' whereabouts or the fact that I've seen them, even when I thought I was being careful. Better to be safe than sorry. I've already messed things up once for my family. I can't risk messing things up twice.

I wish I had my notebook so I could look at the quote on the inside cover, the words floating across the illustrated swans. But I can remember them well enough in my head: *Silence is the means of avoiding misfortune.* If only I knew why I can't see my brothers yet. Maybe no one's supposed to know they live with my grandmother. Maybe that's what the "agreement" is all about. But I'll understand soon. I'll get my birthday present, like Granny P said, as long as I don't slip up.

My birthday is six days away. That's nothing. I can keep my mouth shut until then. If anyone can, I can. The past seven months rush back to me: Green Pasture. The plan. The tally marks. The bubble. I thought it had all been one huge disaster, an experiment gone wrong. But really it had been preparing me for something bigger. All along, without knowing, I'd been training for something important. For this.

I smile. With a burst of new energy, I start walking in the direction I came from, or think I came from. *Why don't you talk, Elise? Why are you so quiet all the time?* Even though I won't be able to answer these questions out loud, I'll have a real reason now. And not just any reason. A good one. My brothers. My family. The woods are dimmer than ever, and my feet heavier than ever, but it's all okay because finally, finally I have an explanation.

It's all okay, I keep telling myself, even as my belly thunders and the woods go on. Even as questions pound in my head. When—if—the woods ever end, where will I come out? Where will I go? I don't see how I can go home. I don't see how I can face my mother, be under the same roof as her, with the way we left things. There was a time when I could have gone to Mel's house. But even if that were an option, it wouldn't be a good idea, not with my promise to Granny P. I'd want to tell Mel everything.

I keep hoping that I'll come across my backpack on the ground somewhere, and that the box of crackers I packed will still be in it. But of course there's no sign of it. There's no sign of anything familiar. Where is that stupid stream? I don't know if I've passed these trees before. All I know is that I need to make it out of these woods before dark. And I need to keep moving, or I might freeze in these damp clothes. It may be spring officially, but winter lingers.

Crack-boom.

A gunshot behind me chills me to my core. I stumble and peer over my shoulder, but the woods are dusky in the weakening light. I hear voices. A dog barking. They're back. I thought I'd escaped them for good.

Crack-boom.

Another gunshot, closer now. I hurl my body away from the sounds. If I let them get me, they'll make me pay for escaping last time. They'll kill me with their guns and bury me in the woods to make sure I never tell anyone what they did and stole. I have to keep running, though I don't know how I'm going to last. How long can a person run on empty?

I push my legs. Any race I run in track will feel like nothing compared to this. That is, if I live to do track again. Onward, breathe, in through the nose, out through the mouth. In through the nose, out through the mouth. The air feels too thin. But the woods are thinning too. The trees are changing, softening into bushes...

And trimmed grass.

And a shining swing set.

I freeze at the edge of the woods. Someone's backyard.

My legs turn to jelly, giving way. I shouldn't have stopped moving.

"Hey." Feet pad against grass somewhere behind me. "Hey!"

The hound must have led the hunters right back to me. My heart hammers in panic. I can practically feel them on top of me again, can feel the boot pressing into my face. I've got to get up before they can grab me and drag me back into the woods. I crawl forward in the grass and glance across the yard at the house. A window glows: a beacon of yellow. Someone must be home. A cry of "help" rises in my throat, but the bubble forms around me, blocking its escape. I try to push through—then I remember: *Don't say a word to anyone.* How could I have forgotten so quickly? The people inside probably wouldn't have heard me anyway. Good thing the bubble is one step ahead of me.

Trust the bubble. That should be my new motto.

A boot plants itself in the grass next to me. I summon my muscles, or what's left of them, and swing around, punching him hard, wherever my fist hits first.

"Aaugh!"

It turns out I hit a private area. He staggers back, clutching himself, his face contorted.

But it's not the buzz-cut boy's face, or either of his buddies'.

"Elise?" Conn Karney squints at me.

I scuttle backward in a crab walk. I won't let my confusion set me off my guard. I feel bad about hitting him, but he'll survive. I need to get away while he's down.

A girl comes running up behind him.

No, not more people. I want fewer. None.

Fin frowns at Conn. "What happened to you?" She looks over at me. "Is that…?"

"Yeah."

"What's she doing here?"

"No clue." Conn leans on his knees, still scrunched up in pain. His binoculars dangle from his neck. "Might be lost. She punched me before I could ask."

Fin walks toward me. "You okay?"

I nod so she'll leave me alone.

"I'm fine too, thanks for asking," Conn mutters.

I stand to show them I'm leaving. They mean well, but I can't afford people talking to me, expecting me to say things. I can't let anyone put me at risk of trying to speak again and breaking my promise. I look past the side of the house toward the front yard. I can see a road and some kind of orchard on the other side. I don't know where I am, but the road will at least take me somewhere. The woods will only get me lost again. Or killed.

As I walk across the yard, the edges of my vision blacken. My legs bend and flop like licorice twists. *Oh no.* I focus on the road ahead. My feet keep crossing in front of each other. The only way to stop it is to sit down. I drop to the ground.

Fin leans over me, feeling my forehead, saying words. "She's burning up. Help me get her inside."

I try to shake my head, but none of me can move. Conn takes my other arm, and as they lift me, I think I must have been reborn back in those woods, because I'm like a newborn. I can't talk, I can't walk, I can barely lift my head.

Newborn. Born new. I let the thought carry me off on its wings.

CHAPTER 13

A SWIRLY OFF-WHITE CEILING. STRIPED wallpaper. A painting of a beach. These are the sights that greet me when I open my eyes.

I prop myself onto my elbows. A lamp glows on the bedside table. Usually I can't sleep with a light on, even a night-light. I must have really been in a bad way. I look around the rest of the room. Aside from the twin bed and the nightstand, a treadmill sits in the middle of the floor, and skis, snowboards, beach chairs, umbrellas, and other stuff are heaped in corners. I look out the window, but it's all dark. What time is it?

I switch the lamp to a brighter setting and pick up the hand mirror lying beside it. Puffy eyes look back at me from under big, uneven eyebrows. A feather is clipped in my hair. The feather… Everything rushes back to me. The cottage, my brothers, Granny P. It's all a little foggy, maybe because I'm still waking up. Did I really see my brothers and talk to Granny P? I touch the feather in my hair; it's as real as anything. As real as the air I'm breathing. As real as the echo of fiddles in my head. The drumming of purpose in my chest...

"You're awake."

I drop the mirror on the bed. Fin stands in the doorway with Conn hovering behind her.

"You should have knocked," Conn murmurs.

Fin ignores him and smiles. "Feeling better? You were out for an hour."

I nod.

"Here." She walks into the room, stepping over the treadmill and some ski gear to hand me a glass of water.

I sit on the edge of the bed and gulp the water down.

"I'd better refill that." She takes the glass back. "You must be hungry too. Dinner'll be ready soon."

Dinner? Too bad I'm not staying for dinner. But they'll figure it out later, when the window's open and I'm gone. I don't know where I'll be, but I won't be here. I'll leave a thank-you note, though.

Fin disappears into the hall, and my nose catches a scent wafting in. My stomach swoons.

Maybe I could stay for one meal. One meal shouldn't

be too bad. Maybe they'll bring me a tray of food so I can eat in here by myself. Besides, I have no money for food, and it's easier to think on a full stomach. I can work out a plan after dinner.

Conn shifts in the doorway. "Sorry about all the junk in here. The spare room's sort of doubling as a storage room, since we keep running out of space. I swear the house is shrinking." He laughs and clears his throat. "So, is everything okay? You looked pretty frazzled earlier. If there's anything you want to talk about..."

I busy myself smoothing out the comforter I was sleeping on. Even if I wanted to talk about something, I couldn't.

"You probably just want a ride home. Your mom must be wondering where you are."

I stop smoothing the comforter and shake my head with a jolt of annoyance. My mother doesn't care where I am. And Conn has brought up the last thing I want to think about: going home to her.

But where else can I go?

"No?" Conn frowns. "You mean she's not home?"

Another head shake. How many can I get away with?

"Okay. When will she be back? One of my parents can take you then."

Dread courses through me. I can't let them take me home. I can't go back to my mother. I glance at a calendar hanging on the wall; a painting of tulips marks the month of April. An idea springs out of my desperation. I don't know if it will work, but I decide to try it. I walk up to the calendar and point to my birthday.

"She's gone till Friday?" Conn's eyebrows rise.

I nod. I don't like lying—that's my mother's specialty—but I'll explain it all to him after my birthday, and he'll understand why I did it.

"I hear we have a visitor," a woman's voice chirps.

I turn to see Fin at the doorway behind Conn, with another glass of water and a pregnant lady in an apron.

"Mom, meet Elise Pileski. Elise, meet Mom." Fin waves a hand between us.

"You'll have to excuse my appearance." Mrs. Karney wipes a streak of flour off her cheek. "I was just getting dinner ready."

I think she's waiting for me to object, to tell her she looks ravishing. When I don't say anything, she blinks and smiles wider. "Can you stay for a bite, dear? I've set a place for you."

"She doesn't really talk," Fin mutters.

"Oh." Mrs. Karney blinks again, but her smile holds. "I see. Well, when are her parents expecting her home? I don't want them to worry."

I almost laugh. I can't imagine my mother worrying about me.

"She lives with her mom," Conn chimes in for me. "But her mom's away till Friday."

"Away?" Mrs. Karney cocks her head. "What for?"

Conn shrugs and looks at me. "Is it a business trip or something?"

At least this one's yes or no. I nod, letting the lie build.

"And who's looking after you while she's away?" Mrs. Karney directs the question at me. I think she's already forgotten what Fin said about me not talking.

I shake my head. It makes no sense as an answer to her question, but what am I supposed to do?

"No one?" Mrs. Karney puts a hand over her heart. "My goodness. She's left you home by yourself?"

I stare at my hands. I don't nod, but I don't shake my head either.

"You'd think she'd hire a sitter, or leave you with a relative, or—"

"Maybe she doesn't have relatives close by," Fin says.

"And why would Elise need a sitter when she's old enough to be one?"

"Well, I don't like it...a young girl alone for almost a week. Especially at night. Do you know how to cook for yourself, Elise?"

It depends on what she means by "cook." I could manage pasta or grilled cheese or canned soup—the sorts of things I've seen my mother make. I've tried my hand at them a few times, on nights when my mother forgot about dinner or went to bed early.

"Mom," Conn says. "Instead of judging someone else's parenting, can't you just let Elise stay here a while?" He glances at me. "Assuming she wants to, of course."

The solution I was hoping for unfolds before me. I'd prefer to avoid people altogether, but there's really nowhere I can go where that's guaranteed. Even if I go back into the woods and sleep in a tree, there are bullies out there. And dogs. And no food. No hot water. If I can stay here, I'll at least have a place to sleep and food to eat, without having to face my mother yet. I can bide my time. And Fin and Conn don't seem to mind me not talking, so maybe it won't be too bad.

Mrs. Karney gasps, offended. "Of course she can stay. The Karney family never turns away a guest." Her voice is too perky. "She's welcome to stay as long as she wants. But I should at least call her mother."

Call my mother? I hadn't anticipated that.

She pulls a phone out of her apron pocket. "What's her cell number, dear?" She smiles at me. When I don't respond, she hands me the phone. "Why don't you just key it in for me?"

They're all watching me, waiting. I can't put in a fake number; Mrs. Karney will know as soon as the wrong person answers or a voice tells her the number isn't recognized. I hold my breath and dial.

Mrs. Karney takes the phone back and listens. I wait, fighting the urge to bite my nails or escape out the window. So much for my lie. When my mother answers—

"Hi, Mrs. Pileski. Annette Karney calling, from 41 Honeydew Road. I have Elise here—she goes to school with my son and daughter—and she'd like to stay with us while you're away this week, if that's all right with you. I have a spare room. Happy to have her. But if there's any issue, don't hesitate to call me back. My number is…"

I breathe out. She's leaving a message. I can't believe my luck. Then again, I should have known it would go to voice-mail. My mother doesn't answer calls from unknown numbers.

Mrs. Karney hangs up. "Well, now that that's settled,

come on down so you can meet the others and get something in that tummy of yours. You look famished."

Others? How many others? Nobody said there would be others.

Maybe I should have gone out the window after all.

"Everyone, this is Elise. Elise, this is everyone." Conn waves at the blur of faces around the table.

"Don't be lazy," says Fin at my right. "Give her names."

"You do it then." Conn shrugs and leans back in his chair.

"Fine." Fin points without looking. "That's Ben. Lucy. Mabel. Stewey…" She goes down one side of the table, then the next. "Dad. Clare. Dónal. And Penny."

"Saved the best for last, huh?" says the tall girl at the end of the table, the one who must be Penny. But I'm looking at the boy with the buzz cut next to her. The one called Dónal.

My stomach twists. He probably thought he'd never see me again. He probably thought, after I got away, that he'd never have to answer for what he did. Maybe he gets away with a lot of things, and that's why he's so surprised to see me sitting here.

His eyes flicker with recognition. He looks away and fiddles with his collar, seeming much less at ease than he was in the woods. It's a small consolation. Maybe he thinks I'm going to rat him out. I would if it weren't for my promise. At least, I hope I would.

"I like your feather." Penny points at my hair. Strangely, I think she means it. This might have made me smile if *he* weren't in the room.

The toddler in the high chair—Ben?—bangs his spoon over and over on his food tray. Mrs. Karney wipes applesauce off his cheek with one hand and rests her other hand on her pregnant belly that's peeking over the tabletop. Nine children seem plenty to me, but I guess she and Mr. Karney don't think so. Now I understand why Conn said they keep "running out of space."

The two younger girls with missing teeth—Lucy and Mabel?—stare at me. The middle boy wearing glasses—Stewey?—looks down at a book in his lap.

"No reading at the table," Mr. Karney says.

Stewey sighs and closes the book. I know the feeling.

Mr. Karney turns to me, stroking his beard. "So, Elise. How do you know our Fin and Conn?"

I dig my nails into my palms under the table. Just what I needed—an open-ended question. The audience falls silent, waiting for me to say my lines.

But some characters don't have lines. Why does everyone assume you need to have lines to be part of the show? What about all the "extras" in the background? Can't I be one of them?

"She goes to public school with us," Fin answers for me. She rubs down a hangnail with the file on her Swiss Army knife.

Mrs. Karney grimaces at the words *public school*. Or maybe at the pocketknife. "Don't do that at the table. You shouldn't have one of those to begin with."

"Why? Because I'm a *girl*?"

Mrs. Karney's lips go thin. "We have company."

The second-smallest Karney—Lucy, maybe—licks her fork and waves it. "When do *I* go to public school?"

"Sweetie, public school's for people who want to be just like everyone else." Mrs. Karney reaches over and taps Lucy's nose. "You're special."

Fin and Conn roll their eyes. Conn passes me the mashed potatoes. "Careful. Pot's hot."

I take the pot. My stomach roars, and I realize how long it's been since I've eaten. I dump a mountain of potatoes onto my plate.

"Why didn't she say thank you?" The other girl with missing teeth—Mabel, I think—tilts her head and stares at me.

"Don't be rude," Fin says.

"But I thought it was rude not to say thank you."

Beads of sweat tickle my temples. There are too many people in this room.

"Shush." Mrs. Karney gives Mabel a warning look and then holds another pot out to me. "How about some roast duck?"

I hesitate. I didn't even know people ate duck.

"It's delicious." Mr. Karney raises his fork to his mouth. "And Dónal here shot these ducks himself." He grins with pride at his oldest son, killing my appetite. "Making good use of that new hunting license."

I shake my head at the pot Mrs. Karney is holding, and she passes it on to Conn, who doesn't take any either. Fin checks her watch. "Hey, Connie boy, shouldn't you have left already?"

"For what?"

"That bird flick."

"Oh." Conn rolls some green beans around with his fork. "I decided to skip it."

The bird documentary was tonight. I'd forgotten all about it.

"You seemed gung ho about it yesterday."

"It was just something to do." He coughs. "Besides, I wanted to make sure Elise was okay."

"Ohhh." Fin glances sidelong at me, one corner of her mouth curving upward. I drop my eyes to my lap, wishing I had a book there like Stewey does. Instead, I feign interest in the flower design on my napkin.

"Why don't one of you give Elise a tour tomorrow?" Mr. Karney says. "Show her around the orchard."

"I would," Fin says, "but I'll be hunkered down all day. Got two tests Monday."

Conn shrugs. "I can do it."

When I'm finally dismissed, I go back to the spare room, climbing over the treadmill and some skis, and open the window. The air cools me briefly. How can I stay here now, knowing Dónal is here too? At least he lives in the basement, with his own private entrance. I remember Conn and Fin mentioning that to Dawn at Patsy's Pastries. It might be easier to avoid him than it would be to avoid my mother at home. But will I be able to stand it, knowing Dónal's so nearby?

Suddenly, six days seems a lot longer than it did when I was leaving the woods. And tomorrow is Sunday—no school as an excuse to be away from the house. Not that I want to go back to school. But at least it means less time here—that is, if I even get to stay. Who knows when my mother will hear Mrs. Karney's message? Will she call back and demand I come home? Or will she be glad to have me off her hands?

"Hey." Fin comes in with a pair of pajamas. "These should fit."

I take them and look at the flamingo pattern.

"Sorry about the design. My great-aunt Geraldine gave them to me."

I raise an eyebrow in amusement.

"She's basically an older version of my mother. They both think girls wear pink and boys wear blue. Blah, blah, blah. Even though they *know* blue's my favorite color." She huffs and shakes her head. "Sorry. Family stuff gets me worked up sometimes."

She turns to leave and then hesitates, looking back at me. "Listen…I don't know what's going on with you. But if you ever need someone to talk to…"

She and Conn are definitely related. I smile and nod a thank-you.

She smiles back. "Get some rest, okay? You must be pooped after meeting my crazy family." She laughs before shutting the door behind her.

Try as I might, I can't see what was laughable about today. All I can see is the cottage and my brothers and Granny P. At least, I can mostly see them. They're still kind of hazy. I pluck the feather from my hair and stare at it. This is all I have—the sole remnant of what happened in the woods. If only I had some footage to replay, a video or a recording I could watch over and over, to remind me of exactly what Granny P said. Since I don't have that, I wish Granny P would at least send me something—a note, a message, a confirmation that I'll get to see my brothers in the end.

But how would she reach me? She doesn't know I'm staying at the Karneys'. And maybe it doesn't matter. Maybe that's what faith is: not needing evidence or a confirmation. I have this feather in my hand. And this fluttering of hope and certainty in my gut. Can that be enough? For now, it has to be.

CHAPTER 14

I SLIP OUT THE FRONT door at ten the next morning. It's the perfect time because all the Karneys have gone to church, except for Conn and Fin, who are still sleeping. I wonder how they got off the hook. Maybe the same way they argued their way out of homeschool. It must have something to do with the "protest" and "nasty fight" they mentioned that first day in Ms. Standish's office.

At the end of the driveway, I take a right onto the road, in the direction that the Karneys' van turned when they left for church. That's the way to town, and once I get there, I'll have my bearings. On my left, the orchard and its rows and rows of small trees shimmer in the sun. I try to count the rows and get up to ten, but then a car zooms by blasting music, and I lose track. I walk about five more minutes before the orchard ends and I start to pass other houses and driveways. Then buildings and parking lots. Then the post office and the bank and Patsy's Pastries, now with fruit tarts and popovers in the window. I don't look too long, or else my stomach might insist on another sticky bun. That's not what I ventured out for.

My feet steer me along the familiar route, turning up the hill onto my street. I pause at the fence by Mel's house. How long ago was it, the last time I saw her sitting on her front steps waiting for me? It feels like years, though I guess it's only been months.

There's movement in one of the windows. I bolt.

Eventually the next and last house, mine, appears at the top of the hill. Nothing has changed, except maybe the grass is higher. The station wagon is gone as expected. My mother will be out—not at church but at the gym. That's been her Sunday-morning routine for as long as I can remember. I doubt it has changed in the couple of days I've been gone.

I take the spare key from under the mat. Inside, the house is calm and cold. My mother hasn't returned Mrs. Karney's voice message. She hasn't come to the Karneys' house to get me. She hasn't given any indication that she cares where I am. Not that I'm surprised.

I go to my room and pack some things in an extra backpack: my school supplies and textbooks, a spare blank notebook to replace my stolen one, my track stuff, and some shirts and jeans and pajamas. Then I grab my toothbrush from the bathroom and walk into the kitchen, where dishes stew in sink water. My mother never leaves dirty dishes. On the table lies an unfinished scarf, the needles and spool of yarn still attached. It's the same one she was knitting before I left, but it doesn't look any longer.

I sit at the table with a pen and a scrap of paper.

Staying with the Karneys this week, in case you haven't checked your voicemail. Need some time away. I almost add, Not that you care, but I put the pen down.

A business card lies nearby. I pick it up.

Hillview Counseling & Psychotherapy

Call us today to make an appointment

Under the second line, there's a note in my mother's hand: April 11, 2:30 p.m. That's this Wednesday.

I put the card back and stand, glancing again at the sink. Bits of food float in the water. Through the window above it, I see the shed door swinging in the wind. My mother never slid the latch back. I turn away, shaking off a pinching feeling in my chest. The house is still. But when I listen for too long, I hear whispers. Echoes. Shouts. Boyish cries ricocheting off the walls. The voices tinkle, rising above the stillness, louder than my thoughts. I clamp my hands over my ears and run—sprint—then seize my bike by the fence.

I'm back at the Karneys' in no time.

When I pull into the driveway, Conn is reading under a tree in the front yard. He looks up, and I wait for him to ask where I snuck off to. Instead, he closes his book and stands. "Ready for your tour?"

Conn's binoculars bounce against his chest as he walks, but so far he hasn't used them. This convinces me even more that they're for show. "Here's our peach and nectarine grove," he says, leading me past row after row of trees. "No fruit this time of year, but see the pinkish buds? They're getting ready to blossom. And the rest from here to the end are apple trees. They'll blossom next month." He gestures at the orchard like a museum tour guide. I hope he doesn't expect a tip. Any money I had is Dónal's now.

"My parents planted the first ones before I was born. They had to wait *years* for the trees to bear fruit." He shakes his head. "All that waiting must have been torture."

Torture. He uses the word so freely. I guess torture is

different for everyone. For him, waiting is torture. For me, sitting at a table full of people is torture. A class discussion is torture. Lunch in the cafeteria is torture. When I think of those things, waiting for a tree to bear fruit doesn't seem bad at all. And when I think of the day my fruit will come—my birthday—I smile a little. My fruit will be worth the wait. My brothers will be worth the wait.

We emerge from the orchard, and Conn nods at a red barn ahead of us. "That's where our cider press is."

White letters loom across the front of the barn: King Karney's Orchard & Cider Mill.

I stop, shading my eyes in the sun. King Karney apple cider? All the grocery stores around here sell it. My mother buys it sometimes. I didn't realize Fin and Conn were *those* Karneys.

"There's a bunch of boring machinery inside," Conn says. "And controlled-atmosphere storage rooms. They preserve apples practically year-round so we can keep making cider. At least, my dad and Dónal work in there. Fin and I prefer to be out in the orchard, pruning or spraying or what have you."

A shape flutters above us. I glance up, my heart fluttering too. But it's just a small, bluish-gray bird. I don't know what I was expecting.

Conn halts. His hands fly to his binoculars, and his

binoculars to the bridge of his nose. "What do we have here?" After a moment, he pulls a small book out of his pocket and flips through it, stopping somewhere in the middle. "Here we go. White-breasted nuthatch. Yep, that's definitely it. *How* cool."

He holds the binoculars out to me, his face all bright. I worry he might take offense if I don't indulge him, so I take the binoculars and peer through them.

"See him? There in that tree next to the mill. He's got the male coloring."

Scanning, I find a bird perched in the crook of a tree branch. His face and underside are white, but a black streak runs over his head and down the nape of his neck toward his blue-gray back and wings.

I lower the binoculars, but Conn waves them back. "Keep watching."

I find the bird again and wonder how long I'll have to watch until Conn is satisfied. I don't want to insult him.

The bird starts to climb up the tree trunk, pecking at the bark a few times. Then he does a one-eighty and descends down the trunk headfirst. I raise my eyebrows in spite of myself.

"Impressive, right?" Conn says. "Nuthatches are known for climbing down trees like that."

I watch the bird move up the underside of a branch before turning back around. He pauses halfway and curves his head to look upward, like an upside-down wolf howling at the moon. His feet must be clinging to that bark for dear life, but he shows no concern. He's confident; I'll give him that. And cute. After he goes up and down a few more times, I hand the binoculars back to Conn.

"They're quite the little acrobats." He drops his book on the ground. "Let me see if I can get a better look."

He wanders off, and I pick up the book: *Pocket Field Guide to Birds of Eastern North America*. The cover is creased down the middle, the corners frayed. I flip through the sections: "Kingfishers and Trogons." "Swifts and Swallows." "Hummingbirds." "Pigeons and Doves." Each page shows an image of a bird and a short description. "Cuckoos, Anis, and Roadrunners." "Shorebirds." "Ducks, Geese, and Swans."

I slow, scanning the pages. "Trumpeter Swan." "Bewick's Swan." "Whistling Swan." I stop on a page near the end of the section. "Mute Swan. Species: *Cygnus olor*." There's a picture of a swan wholly white in plumage, with an orange bill and a black knob above it. Just like the illustration in my now-lost notebook.

"Swans, huh?"

I jump. Conn is peering over my shoulder. "It's a misno-mer, you know. 'Mute swan.'"

I resume flipping so as not to seem interested in any one page.

"They're not actually mute. They're capable of making sounds. Just less vocal than other swans."

I close the book and hold it out to Conn.

"Nah, you keep it." He taps his temple. "It's all up here anyway."

He meanders off again, and I raise an eyebrow at his back. What is he, some kind of bird expert? As he follows a new bird with his binoculars, I turn back to the page I folded down—the picture of an elegant neck and white feathers and a black mark reaching from each eye toward the bill. The mark, I realize, looks a little like eyebrows that almost meet in the middle. I trace it with my finger. *Capable of making sounds...less vocal...* I smile. If I were to have a Patronus like in Harry Potter, or a dæmon like in His Dark Materials, maybe it would take the form of a mute swan.

I start to close Conn's book, but my fingers linger, thumbing the pages. Something makes me flip a little further.

Owls. Hawks and Vultures. Jays, Crows, and Allies. Blue Jay...Magpie...American Crow...

Common Raven. Species: Corvus corax.

As I land on an image of a stately black bird, its beady eyes seem to be staring straight at me. I snap the book shut and hurry after Conn.

CHAPTER 15

C ALL ME THE FEATHER queen.

I've been wearing the feather in my hair all morning. I get strange looks as I walk the halls of Green Pasture, even more than I did before, but that's to be expected. No one likes being left out of a secret. It's nice having a secret, a mission no one here knows about. My mission will succeed, and if that means I have to take certain measures, then so be it. Mr. Gankle, for example, is making everyone give a research presentation, and I was due to present during second period, so I spent the hour reading in a bathroom stall. Some people might call that cutting class. I call it keeping my promise.

In the library now, I scratch tally marks into my new notebook. I'm not counting words anymore because there are none to count. The tallies stand for something different: a countdown to my birthday, the number of days left. Current count, including today: five tally marks. Four vertical lines with one line across them. There'll be satisfaction in writing fewer marks every day, just like with my old tally.

Even though so much has changed over the weekend, nothing has changed at school. There's still nothing green-pasturey about Green Pasture. The walls in the hallways are still burnt orange, and the fluorescent lights still induce headaches. Bernard Billows and the librarian are still the only other people in the library at lunch. They don't bother me. The three of us have an understanding, I think. Neither of them asks why I'm "quiet," and I don't ask why Bernard Billows never washes his hair, or why the librarian—I still don't know her name—has a Peter Pan tattoo on her arm. We let each other be. I wish the lunch hour would never end.

It always does.

I leave the library and head to English class, tripping and almost falling when I see Beady on Miss Looping's desk.

I was wrong; one thing has changed at Green Pasture.

"First, thank you to whoever returned Beady," Miss Looping says. "It would be nice if you could replace my mug too. But I'll take what I can get."

I peer at Beady through my eyelashes. There are twenty other students in this room, and yet his stare fixes on me. He doesn't move a feather. He thinks he's fooling everyone, but not me. Any doubts I had about what happened that day, after I slammed my book shut and ran off, are gone. He wasn't stolen.

Why did he come back to school? Why today?

I wished Granny P would send me something—a message, a confirmation. Could this be it? I think of the raven on Granny P's shoulder. Is he here to keep an eye on me, to make sure I don't forget my promise?

Miss Looping finishes writing something on the board and turns. *Ghazal*. She taps the word with her finger, smudging the chalk. "Each of you will write a ghazal."

"Uh…" Arty Pilger raises his hand, screwing in his invisible light bulb. "I don't know what that is."

"It was in your reading last night." Miss Looping surveys the blank stares around the room and sighs. "Look it up. It's a type of poem with at least five couplets. It will be a graded assignment and considered for the Green Pasture poetry contest."

Others groan, but I have no complaints. Anything that's not a class presentation or a group project is fine by me.

"And you'll read it aloud to the class."

My jaw tightens. Is she joking? I thought she was on my side.

I was wrong; two things have changed at Green Pasture. I sit clenching my teeth for the rest of class. Why is she doing this to me? Does she think I'm the one who "borrowed" Beady and broke her mug?

When the bell rings, I'm torn between storming out and lingering until everyone leaves, to see if Beady will do anything. If he'll drop the pretense. But the thought of being alone with him puts butterflies in my stomach. What if he *does* move? What if he flies out the window again? Miss Looping really needs to start closing it. It doesn't matter anyway because one kid is staying behind to make up a quiz, and Miss Looping is talking to another student at her desk. I take my books and hurry past them and Beady.

In the hall, I turn the corner toward my locker and bump into someone with neon-green streaks in her hair. I keep my eyes down and try to scoot by. But then there are more people, more shades of the rainbow. I look up. The girl with green hair stares at me.

"Hi."

Mel?

Matching green eye shadow draws out the green in her eyes, which flit over my new hair accessory. This is the first time I've seen her wear makeup.

Make that three things that have changed.

"Nice feather," Sylvia says behind her, sporting hot-pink hair streaks and eye shadow. She glances in amusement above my right ear, where I've fastened the feather with a barrette.

And just like that, it's back to reality. Back to Sylvia's insults masquerading as compliments, going strong since that second day of school when she called a poem of mine "cute." When I was naive enough to think she was being nice. When I was discovering how it feels to be around Mel's friends. It still feels that way, except now everyone's hair and eyelids look different. Theresa's are purple and Nellie's orange. I glance down and notice their nails have been painted their respective colors and manicured—not bitten to uneven lengths like mine.

"Too bad you missed the sleepover Saturday." Sylvia flips her pink locks with her pink fingers. "It was a ton of fun. We gave each other makeovers."

I glance at Mel, but she walks past me. I catch a whiff of chemicals—nail polish, cosmetic fumes, a stranger's scent. Sylvia and the others move with her like a flock of tropical birds, passing before I have to worry about evading a response.

I turn and pull my books closer to my chest. It's going to be a long five days.

Please be a dear

Leave your shoes here

The doormat in the Karneys' foyer welcomes me after track practice. I do its bidding and take off my sneakers, my body buzzing with a sense of achievement. I did it. A whole school day without a word. If I were doing my old tally, this would be a big deal. Of course, now it won't be enough—I have a more important zero to get to, the one that will mean I can see my brothers. Still, it's a small victory.

I don't hear any activity in the house, but I err on the side of caution and steal down the hall and up the stairs as quickly and soundlessly as possible. That's a tricky task with these floors, which groan in certain places, but I've had years of practice in light-footedness at my house. Even though the Karney house is probably as old as mine, the air smells different—like clean laundry. I can't help noticing the lack of mustiness. I step on a Lego piece at the top of the stairs and wince. There's no lack of toys, though.

En route to the spare room, I hear Conn and Mrs. Karney talking in Conn's room.

"I think she should stay with someone else."

"What? I thought you were fine with her staying till her mom gets back. It's only a few more days."

I pause and press my ear to the door.

"There's something... I don't know... She rubs me the wrong way. Never laughs. Never says thank you."

"I told you she's shy."

"Shy?" I hear Mrs. Karney's pregnant shuffle. "That's more than shy. She has a tongue, doesn't she? She never uses it. Just sits there all silent and secretive, like she's hiding something. For all we know, she could be plotting to—"

"Oh, come on. Does she look like an ax murderer to you?"

"Of course she doesn't *look* like one. They don't always look like one. And it's the quiet ones you have to watch out for."

I thought Dónal was the Karney I had to worry about, but maybe I should add Mrs. Karney to the list.

"She never gets in anyone's way. What about all that stuff they tell you in church? Love thy neighbor or whatever. I thought you were all for that."

Mrs. Karney snorts. "Don't preach to me. You're the last person who should be talking about church. You and your sister. You should hear them at Mass. 'Where are Conn and Finola today?' I have to make excuses for you, week after week. It's embarrassing. And now that you've wrangled your way into public school…"

"You're changing the subject."

Mrs. Karney huffs. "All right, listen, I don't want to be the bad guy here. I'm a Good Samaritan. Elise can stay if she wants to. I trust my children, so I trust who they trust."

I step back from the door and slip into the spare room just as I hear Conn's door screech open. Then creaks on the stairs. Then, below me, the simultaneous slams of the kitchen door and the back door. I move to the window and watch Conn walk across the backyard to the tire swing, where Fin is swinging. He says something that makes her laugh and stick out her tongue.

Mrs. Karney is right. Neither of them has any reason to trust me or stick up for me. But they do anyway. Relief mingles with guilt. And gratefulness.

They talk for a bit, and I try to read their lips and hand gestures, but I can't decipher their conversation. I suspect it has to do with me, or maybe Mrs. Karney.

Mrs. Karney, who's nothing like my mother, but at the same time, nothing like Mel's mother. I spent years watching Mrs. Asimakos coddle Mel, hardly ever seeing them butt heads, but it turns out not all other mothers act like that. It turns out I'm not the only kid who can't seem to click with mine.

But Fin and Conn at least have each other.

After a few minutes, they play catch. I lie down, stare at the ceiling, and wish myself to Friday, to my birthday, and to even further beyond that. To a day when Eustace and Emerson and I might be lounging in a field somewhere, having a picnic or playing cards and joking around, commiserating about our mother and how she abandoned us—my brothers physically, and me in every other sense. Because the more time I spend at the Karneys, the more I can't wait to be with my brothers. The more I see that siblings can transcend all the other stuff and give each other something a kid can't always find with a parent.

But since my birthday is still days away, all I can do for now is close my eyes and go back to the yellow cottage in the woods. I go over the details of it in my head—the laughter, the music, my brothers, Granny P—so they won't slip away. So they won't become fuzzier and fuzzier, like other memories have always done. Because right now they're all I have. I just have to get to Friday.

But I have a feeling Mrs. Karney won't make that easy.

CHAPTER 16

I T ALL COMES DOWN to the first thing you think of when you wake up. That first image or idea before the filtering of conscious thought takes over, while you're still in between. Whatever you think of, that's the reason you get up in the first place. That's the reason you get out of bed, into your clothes, into your shoes, and out the door.

This morning, the first thing I think of is them. Their two faces. Their wheelchairs. Their laughter. Their music. What they must have suffered through—the accident, the pain, my mother's abandonment. I keep racking my brain for possible reasons why my mother would disown her sons. And I keep coming back to my initial suspicion: that she didn't want the burden, the expense of disabled children. Maybe at first in her fragile state of mourning my father and trying to nurse a new baby, she truly couldn't handle caring for them, and Granny P had agreed to take them in the meantime. And maybe it was only supposed to be a temporary arrangement, but then my mother, for whatever selfish reason, never took my brothers back—refused to. I know I shouldn't think the worst of people, but my mother has never shown me her best.

In a way, though, it doesn't matter why she sent them away. What matters is that my brothers are okay. Everything is going to be okay. And their music, their laughter, their faces, the prospect of being with them, doing sibling things, speaking a sibling language—it gets me out of bed and ready to face another day at Green Pasture.

I check that my feather's in place as I take my seat in first period. It's starting to look more like a feather skeleton since little pieces keep falling off, but I leave it clipped in my hair for good luck. I don't even care when people stare anymore.

Mr. Gankle waves a wad of papers at us. "I've graded your research presentations. Great work, everyone."

He strolls around the room and hands out our evaluation sheets, pausing at my desk. "Elise." He sets my sheet in front of me. "You didn't come to class on your presentation date."

I look down at the box labeled "Grade." There's a zero next to the percent sign.

"If you were sick, I need a doctor's note, and then we can find you another day to present."

I nod, even though no doctor will write me a note for reading in a bathroom stall.

He sighs. "I'd hate for you to keep this zero when you've done so well on your other assignments."

People have committed murders and felonies, and he's after me for not giving a class presentation? Teachers need to get their priorities straight. Miss Looping used to be an escape from adults like Mr. Gankle, but now even she has assigned a presentation. It's too bad there are no more teachers left to like.

As soon as Mr. Gankle moves on to another student, I scan his syllabus and the grading breakdown. *Research Presentation: 5%*. I exhale. That's nothing. I can still manage an A-minus in this class, even with that zero. As long as it's the only zero.

I turn my evaluation sheet upside down and touch my feather. Zero is a funny number. It means something good when it comes to my tallies. When it comes to grades, not so much. But when I think of my brothers, things like grades seem small.

The clouds let it rip for the first track meet. Puddles are already forming on the track. Ponchos and umbrellas crowd the bleachers, some of them belonging to strangers here for the visiting team and others to Green Pasture students, parents, maybe even teachers—but I'm trying not to look. I'm trying not to think about all those eyes that will be watching me, or the fact that this isn't just a practice anymore. That this is what we've been practicing *for*.

When the runners for the mile race are called, a tingling feeling starts in my butt and spreads all over my body. I'm going to be sick, very sick. How can I run when I'm going to be sick?

I go to my mark anyway and wait for the gun. Coach Ewing gives me a thumbs-up. What if I trip? What if I run out of stamina in the first lap? What if I forget to breathe in through my nose, out through my mouth, and to keep my arms parallel, and to relax my hands, and then I come in last? What if—?

Crack!

The starter pistol goes off, and bodies shoot forward. A girl from the other team breaks into a sprint. I remember what Coach Ewing said about runners like her. She's going to use up all her energy in the first lap and fall behind. I can't let it bother me that she's already so far ahead.

I pace myself. In the second lap, I pick it up a little, but only a little. I see Mel and Sylvia watching on the sidelines—their event is the two-mile—and this makes me go a little faster. In the third lap, I pass a few runners on my team. Then a few on the other team. I glance over at the soccer field next to the track, but it's a blur of shapes.

In through the nose, out through the mouth. Relax hands. Arms forward and backward.

At least six runners are ahead of me. The sprinter is still in the lead. Coach Ewing said those people fall behind in the second lap, maybe the third, but now we're going into the final lap, and she's still ahead.

But she's struggling. She's working harder to maintain her pace.

I lengthen my stride. I pass a runner from the other team, then another. Now there are three people between me and the sprinter. The faces on the sidelines rush by me, or I rush by them. My lungs are burning. I hear shouts. "You've got this!" "Go, Elise!" I catch a blur of neon-green hair. Mel's talking to someone, not Sylvia...Fin? I can't waste energy looking around. My legs rev, propelling me forward past the next runner, and the next, and the next. They're all clumped in a pack, but beyond them it's just the sprinter. I fix my eyes on her back. I can see her arms swinging from side to side, her hands clenched in fists. Bad form. She's tired.

I'm tired too. I can't feel my legs. They move under me like wheels hydroplaning.

But hydroplaning is kind of like flying. There's no sense of traction. Like I'm close to knowing what it's like to be a bird.

I'm a swan, and my legs are throbbing wings.

No one would expect the quiet one to pass the sprinter. No one would expect the quiet one to win. No one expects much of anything from the quiet one.

I thrust my chest forward, reaching, hurling myself across the finish line. I fall to my knees. Coach Ewing runs toward me with a timer, but I can't hear what she's saying because all the blood and adrenaline are rushing to my head. My lungs beg for air.

"Six minutes, two seconds, kid. Second place." Coach Ewing bends down and thwacks me on the back. "And first for Green Pasture." I don't have the strength to nod in acknowledgment. All I know is that I didn't pass the sprinter. I missed her by a feather.

"Listen, we need you in the four-by-four relay next time. You up for it? We need our fastest runners for that race." Coach

Ewing thumps my back again and walks away, flipping through her clipboard papers and calling out to other teammates.

I stretch my legs, fighting the numbness in them, and then drain my water bottle.

They need me in the relay, she said. So this is how it feels to be needed. Living with my mother, I've gone years without knowing the feeling. Apparently Mel doesn't need me anymore either. But now Coach Ewing needs me. The track team needs me. And for reasons I'll find out soon, my brothers need me—and Granny P needs me—to keep my promise. When someone is needed, that means they're vital. I've always wanted to be vital.

I'm in a pretty good mood when I reach the Karneys' after the track meet. I even feel like whistling as I get off my bike. I don't, though, in case someone hears. *Oh, she'll whistle, but she won't talk?* Mrs. Karney would say. *That's exactly what an ax murderer would do.* So instead I just think-whistle. That is, until I open the front door and walk into Dónal.

He's wearing his hunting gear, including a camouflage baseball cap that says "Born to Hunt." Classy. I want more than anything to turn around and get back on my bike, but I can't give him the satisfaction.

He nods at me, shotgun in hand. "Nice day for a walk."

Is he really trying to make small talk?

I stand in the narrow foyer waiting for him to back up or move aside so I can get by.

"Do you mind getting out of my way?" He takes a step toward me, and I catch a whiff of spearmint on his breath—the scent of the gum I had in the backpack he stole from me. "My buddies are waiting for me in the woods."

Of course people are only in *his* way, never the other way around. But I just want him to be gone, so I step aside and press my back to the wall.

"Thanks a million." The corner of his mouth twitches ever so slightly. "I'll tell Mark and Dakota you say hi. Unless you wanna join us?"

I glare at him. For someone in a hurry, he's taking his sweet time.

"What? You didn't have fun with us last time?" He smirks. "Suit yourself. Should be a good day for wildfowl."

My heart skips a beat. *Wildfowl.* Birds.

As Dónal moves past me, I picture him and his pals out there, chomping on my gum and cackling and shooting thoughtlessly at the sky. At innocent creatures. At Conn's little nuthatch, or a mute swan...or Granny P's companion. I imagine a bullet striking, a *kraaa* of pain, a dark shape falling. Falling…

I lunge toward Dónal. My hands reach out and wrench the shotgun from his grasp.

He spins around on the threshold, his mouth falling open. This is the last thing he expected of me. And the last thing I expected of myself. I grip the weapon, not sure what the next step is. Run? Hide the gun somewhere so he can't use it? I should have thought this through.

"What's going on?"

Fin's voice. She appears with Conn on the front steps behind Dónal. Their eyes swivel from Dónal to me to the gun in my hand.

"What does it look like?" Dónal laughs hoarsely and holds up his hands. "Come on, you don't really want to do this, do you?"

I look at the gun, which happens to be pointed at Dónal.

"Listen, just put it down," Dónal says in his most convincing victim voice. "You don't want to hurt anybody. You don't belong in jail."

Heat rips across my face. Fin and Conn don't actually buy his act, do they? *He's* the one who belongs in jail. I look back at Fin, whose eyes have narrowed to slits of suspicion.

I can't bring myself to look at Conn, in case his eyes have narrowed too. Not that I'd blame him. This would be a good time to say something. *I wasn't... I didn't...*

But their eyes on me are muddling my thoughts, closing up my throat. I can feel the bubble sealing me in. Then Granny P's voice echoes in my head: *Don't say a word to anyone.* Louder, louder. *Don't say a word to anyone.*

Before I know what I'm doing, I drop the gun and flee upstairs.

In the spare room, I realize I'm soaked with sweat. Why can't I think before I act? Why did I have to grab the gun? It might not have been so bad if I could have explained myself. Did Granny P really mean for me not to say a word even at times like this? The bubble seems to think so. It scares me a little, how strong the bubble's become. *Trust the bubble*, I remind myself. I guess it's like a safety net, safeguarding my promise. I don't want to jeopardize my chances of seeing my brothers. But I also don't want Fin and Conn, who've only been nice to me, to think I pointed a gun at their brother on purpose.

Maybe there's a way to fix this without speaking. I knock over a pair of skis and trip over the treadmill as I fumble for paper and a pen. Now that I'm away from Fin's and Conn's stares and Dónal's smug expression, I can think a little straighter.

He was going to shoot birds, I write. That's why I took the gun from him. That's all.

I shouldn't be writing notes. Granny P didn't say writing was off limits, but after that social media disaster, I know the trouble it could cause. Even written messages can be misunderstood. But right now this is the only way I can get Fin and Conn to know the truth.

Conn's bedroom door is half open. I glimpse his leg dangling from his bed. Before I can change my mind, I slip the note under his door, making sure the paper rustles audibly, and then hurry back to the spare room.

A minute passes. Then another. What if the note wasn't clear enough? Should I have explained more? Will he believe me? Did I just make things worse? It's like I never learn...

The note reappears under my door.

I hold my breath and pick it up.

I hate that he hunts. I've tried to stop him
too, lots of times. Never works.

I breathe out. Conn's still on my side.

I take my pen and jot down one more thing: Please tell Fin.

I should probably be writing this to Fin herself. But writing to Conn feels easier for some reason, kind of like talking to him at Patsy's Pastries felt easier, before Fin and Dawn joined us. If only we were discussing pizza and poetry again now, and not this.

My hand hovers over the note, tempted to add: *Dónal isn't who you think he is. He did something in the woods...* But I put the pen down and sneak back to Conn's door to drop off the new note.

I'm surprised when another note arrives. I thought we were done.

See you at dinner.

Dinner. The last thing I want to do is go to dinner. But if I don't go, I'll look guilty. And go to bed hungry. That's another one of Mrs. Karney's house rules, and my least favorite: Everyone eats meals together. If you don't eat at the table when dinner is served, you don't eat.

When I take my place at the table later, Dónal is sitting in his spot next to Penny, talking and laughing and chewing with his mouth open like nothing happened. I glance at Fin. Her eyes stay on her food.

Mrs. Karney babbles about a new pregnancy diet she's trying, and Mr. Karney is saying "uh-huh," though I don't think he's listening. I guess they haven't been told about the incident. I keep thinking Dónal is going to say something about it. I keep dreading the moment. But he doesn't mention it. Maybe our encounter in the woods is still hanging over his head. Or maybe he wants this hanging over *my* head.

When I'm asked the occasional question—*Would you like some salad, Elise?* or *So I hear you're on the track team?*—I get by with nods, head shakes, and gestures. The younger Karneys still stare at me, but I guess they don't know any better, and I ignore them the same way I ignore Dónal. Fin keeps stabbing at her chicken and doesn't speak to me or look over at me. She doesn't even pass the mashed potatoes. She puts them down on their way around the table, just out of my reach, because she knows I won't ask for them. And I realize then that I've lost some of her trust, or maybe all of it, and no note I write will be enough to get it back.

CHAPTER 17

Things could be worse. You could be...

- A prisoner in a labor camp
- The match girl who freezes to death in that fairy tale
- A blobfish at the bottom of the ocean

Y OU'LL SEE SEVERAL CHARACTER types in these plays," Miss Looping is saying. "For example, ghost characters and unseen characters." I glance up at the board, where she's writing notes about Shakespeare that I'm supposed to be copying. Her class feels especially long today. Maybe it's because Beady's stare keeps boring into me. Or because Miss Looping keeps reminding us that our ghazal presentations are coming up. I'm starting to understand why people think she's weird. Her arms move so awkwardly, and her velvet dresses are so tacky. I bet she has no life outside of teaching. I bet she has no friends and lives alone with a bunch of cats.

Well, that's what she gets for assigning a presentation.

"Anyone know what a ghost character is?"

To no one's surprise, Arty Pilger raises his hand.

"Yes, Arty?"

"If I had to guess, a ghost character is a ghost."

Students in the back laugh.

Miss Looping displays her always-patient smile. "It does sound like that, doesn't it? By definition, though, a ghost character isn't literally a ghost." She proceeds to write the definition on the board:

Ghost character: a character who is indicated as being onstage but doesn't say or do anything except enter and perhaps exit

I pause in my list-making and stare at the board.

doesn't say or do anything except enter and perhaps exit

Now that's more like it. That's who I'd be in a show. There's a part for me after all. I'd have gotten along swimmingly in Shakespeare's day.

"Keep in mind that ghost characters are generally viewed as editing mistakes," Miss Looping says. "They signify unresolved revisions to the text. The ghost character in *Timon of Athens*, for instance, is thought to demonstrate the play's unfinished state. Not to be confused with unseen characters, which are…" Miss Looping rambles on, but I'm not listening.

A ghost character is a mistake, an imperfection.

Thanks a lot, Miss Looping. Thanks for letting me know.

When the bell rings, I make a beeline for the door.

"Elise."

I stop and turn as other students skirt around me. Miss Looping smiles and beckons me toward her desk.

I stand there for a moment, wishing I'd kept walking—I could have been halfway down the hall by now—and then reluctantly move toward her desk.

"I thought of a few more poets you might like," she says. "Have you read any Poe or Tennyson?"

How can she pretend to act all nice after what she just said? I shake my head and glare past her at the wall.

Miss Looping's smile falters in the corner of my vision. She leans forward on her elbows. "Is…everything all right? You looked upset today."

Her question catches me off guard. I blink and meet

her eyes—warm bursts of chocolate. The bubble that's been encircling me all day quivers for a second, like it might pop.

Then I remember she just called me a mistake. On top of assigning a presentation. I don't need her concern or her poetry recommendations. And I have a promise to keep. I nod with a stiff neck and turn away, feeling Beady's gaze on my back.

Eating in the library is an acquired skill.

I sit at my table near the poetry stacks, my book of sonnets open in front of me. I feel for my sandwich on my lap—Mrs. Karney's ham and apple butter—and watch the librarian. As soon as she turns her back, I bring the sandwich up for a bite. When she turns again, I slip it back under the table and drop my eyes to my book. QUIET IN THE LIBRARY isn't the only sign here, after all; the other one says NO FOOD. The trick is to not take too big a bite in case she looks up before I've swallowed. Chipmunk cheeks would be a dead giveaway.

"You're good at that."

I freeze mid-chew and turn. Conn is standing behind me.

"So this is where you hang out. I'd been wondering why I never see you in the cafeteria."

Why is he here, ruining my routine?

He moves to the chair opposite me. "Can I join you?"

I look around. There are a dozen other tables he could sit at, all empty. At the same time, it seems silly to pretend we're strangers—to shake my head no, he can't join me, when he's been sticking up for me at his house. But if he sits down, he's going to want to chitchat, as people who aren't strangers do. Because we aren't strangers anymore, whether I like it or not.

This is why I shouldn't make friends. It could jeopardize my promise.

Conn hesitates. "I won't bother you, I swear. Just trying to catch up on some work. I have trouble studying at my house because, you know, it's chaos." He laughs.

"Hey there." The librarian pops up behind Conn, whispering. I clamp my hands over my sandwich under the table. "This is a quiet workspace, okay? Students are trying to work."

My muscles relax a little. I like her. We're on the same page—even if the only other student here is Bernard Billows, who's snoozing in the opposite corner.

Conn holds up his hands and mouths, *Sorry*.

The librarian nods, seeming satisfied. Then she glances at me, her lips curving into a smile before she twirls on her heel and returns to her bookshelves. I think that's the closest she and I have come to interacting.

Conn takes the seat across from me. His binoculars clonk against the table. He winces and mouths, *Sorry*, again. He spreads out all his textbooks and notes, and I spot a list of words that look like Italian. I wonder if the Italian teacher cares less about oral exams and practicing conversations than Mrs. Bebeau does. Maybe I should have taken Italian instead of French.

He pulls out his sandwich—also ham and apple butter, by the looks of it—and tries to mimic my technique, glancing at the librarian before whipping his sandwich up to his mouth and then down again under the table. He swallows a bite and takes a bow of triumph in his chair. I guess he's not bad for an amateur—barring the big smear of apple butter on his chin.

I look at him and tap my own chin. He wipes his face with the back of his hand, missing the apple butter by an inch. *Gone?* he mouths. I give him a thumbs-up and return to my book, trying to keep my face straight. It's official: the library is no longer the safe, neutral place it was yesterday.

And I don't mind as much as I thought I would.

I decide to make a detour after track practice today. Instead of going straight to the Karneys', I head to my street. This time, I force myself not to look at Mel's house as I pass it biking up the hill. The only time I see Mel now is during practices, but I won't be going to those anymore. Coach Ewing made me do a four-by-four relay today with Mel, Sylvia, and Nellie to prepare for our next meet. Sylvia did a bad handoff, scratching me with her pink nails and causing me to drop the baton. I suspect she did it on purpose; I heard the three of them snickering about it after. There's no reason to stay on the team when I can run on my own. That's the nice thing about running. It requires me alone.

When I reach my house, I inch up the drive. The station wagon isn't here. It's safe to go inside and write a note.

But now that I'm here, I can't go in. I can't see how many more dishes have piled up in the sink. I can't hear those whispers and echoes again.

I get off my bike, find a pen and a pad of sticky notes in my backpack, and write the note outside. Still staying with the Karneys. Should be back sometime Friday. I lift the pen and then bring it down again, adding, School's good.

I press the sticky note to the front door and pick up my bike.

The distant crunch of tires on gravel startles me. I fling myself and my bike behind a bush, just before the station wagon crests the hill and pulls into the driveway.

My mother gets out of the car carrying grocery bags, her head turned away from me. She sneezes. I wait, but no one else is here to say "bless you," so her sneeze hangs in the air, unblessed. One of the grocery bags slips from her hand. She stares at it as if contemplating whether it's worth the reach and then finally stoops and retrieves it. I watch her trudge up the walk to the front door, set down her bags, and fumble with her keys. She lifts her eyes and pauses, peering at my note on the door. I hold my breath while she peels it off. I want to look away, but my gaze sticks to her back. She stands there for a minute, not moving. Then she turns around and sits on the front step. As she looks at the note, her eyes seem to sink back within purplish rings. Purpler than the last time I saw her. Does the unsleep visit her too?

She shuts her eyes and presses the note to her nose. If I didn't know any better, I'd think she was smelling it.

Is she smelling it?

I hug my knees to my chest.

She hugs hers to her chest. We stay like this, hugging.

I blink, and water gleams on her cheeks. I focus on being still and blending in with the bush.

Another few blinks, and my mother is standing, opening the door, retreating. The taste of salt coats my lips.

CHAPTER 18

A NEW COLOR HAS JOINED the Flock.

That's what I call them now since they only ever move as one. As Conn and I leave the library, full of today's ham and apple butter sandwiches, the Flock comes down the hall. Pink, purple, orange, green...and the new one, blue. Mel is talking to her: a girl with aqua-blue streaks in her reddish-brown hair.

"Fin?" Conn frowns.

Fin slows as she and the Flock approach. "Oh, hey."

"What did you do to your hair?"

Fin shrugs. "Just a little change."

"Have Mom and Dad seen it?"

"Not yet."

"They'll flip."

"Good."

She must have done it last night after dinner and left the house early this morning. I didn't see her at breakfast.

Sneaky. Her nails and eyelids are still plain, so maybe she's easing herself in.

She locks eyes with me and then snaps her head back to Mel. When did they become friends? I guess it shouldn't be surprising; they're in the same grade and on the track team together. I stare at them in spite of myself. Mel doesn't give me the time of day. Hot-pink Sylvia, on the other hand, is smirking her usual smirk. "Feather's thriving, I see." Her eyes swivel from me to Conn. "This your new boyfriend?"

My cheeks catch fire. Conn coughs.

"Interesting pair." Sylvia cocks her head. "Binoculars Boy and Feather Girl. Cute and Mute."

Behind Sylvia, I see Fin's mouth twitch. Nellie and Theresa press their lips together. Mel looks at the floor.

What did I ever do to Sylvia? Well, I guess I spilled the beans about her parents' split in front of everyone, but that was months ago, and I didn't know it was a secret. Is she ever going to stop punishing me for that? It's safe to say I learned my lesson.

She walks past us, and Mel and the others follow. "See you later," Fin mumbles to Conn over her shoulder, before she and the Flock disappear around the corner.

"Huh." Conn stares after her. "Fin has new friends. *How* interesting."

He doesn't comment on what Sylvia called us. Called me. But I know he heard it. The *M* word. It might be worse than the Q word.

Conn and I part ways for fourth period, and as soon as I get to French class, I pull out my notebook.

My silence does not define me. My silence does not define me. I write it all over the covers, front and back. The inside and the outside.

My silence does not define me. My silence does not define me.

Since I'm done with the track team, I head to the library after the last bell instead of to practice. I walk down the hall toward the inviting block letters. QUIET IN THE LIBRARY. I smile at them as I slip through the double doors.

I halt at the sight of chairs in rows. And people sitting in them—some students, but mostly teachers and other adults. At the far end of the library, a podium has been set up. I don't see Bernard Billows or the librarian anywhere.

Then I notice the sign.

Green Pasture Community Poetry Series

Thursday, April 12, 2:30 p.m.

I glance at the clock on the wall. Two twenty-nine. I hurry back toward the doors.

"Thank you all for coming. It's my honor to introduce our first reader and published poet, Green Pasture's own Lenore Looping."

I look over my shoulder. The librarian stands at the podium.

"I've known Lenore since our college days, and I'm still in awe of her talent. She's been published in five anthologies, and today she'll be reading from her first book of poems, *The Shadow Sister*."

Miss Looping rises from a chair in the front row and comes to the podium. Thin curls quiver around her face. "Thank you, Jenna." Her eyes avoid the audience. "The first piece I'll read for you is a shape poem. For those who aren't familiar, it's shaped like its subject matter." She holds up a piece of paper. The text on the page forms the profile of a woman's face. "This one I wrote two summers ago, about my sister's suicide." She clears her throat.

I stand by the doors, my head still turned over my

shoulder. I watch her eyes, sunken but focused, move across the woman's profile, across the lines of the poem. I watch her hands motion gracelessly but firmly. "'There's a shadow of you I found, then lost. I saw it by the guitar box. I'd ask you why you left it there, but you left too. You left too…'"

I watch her start to glow—to stand taller as her voice grows louder. People in the audience nod, close their eyes, or lean forward in their seats.

"'…you left, you went, without your shadow, and now it's mine to bear. Now it's mine to wear…'"

A dry spot on my throat tickles. I swallow, trying to force it away, but it makes me cough. A man glares at me.

"'…but you always preferred to be a shadow. You always preferred that, didn't you…'"

Another cough rises. I try to swallow it again, but it escapes. "Shh," someone hisses. Now is not the time for a coughing fit. I'm ruining Miss Looping's poem, ruining her moment.

I'm glad to be standing in the back. I slip out the double doors, coughing and sputtering and stumbling for a drinking fountain. I can't find one. I guess I've never looked for one. I never look up from my feet. I never look—really look—at the things around me, the people walking by, because I'm so focused on getting away from them. I wonder what else I've missed, besides Miss Looping's poetry.

I didn't know she had a sister.

Her classroom is empty but for Beady. I hurry past him without meeting his eyes and sit at a desk in the back row, coughing until the tickle subsides. I open my notebook and flip past pages of tally marks.

Ghazal due Friday.

I can feel Beady hovering at the other end of the room, staring, challenging me.

As I think of Miss Looping standing at the podium, reading from that woman's profile, I have a strange urge to reach her. Someone. Anyone.

I bring the pen down. I don't lift my eyes, not even when I think I hear a ruffling of feathers, because I know that if I do, I'll lose my concentration, lose the words gushing out of my pen. By the time I scribble the last word, Mr. Koptev is wheeling his cleaning cart into the room. I look up, but Beady is standing still. Of course—he isn't going to move now that the janitor's here. I grab my stuff and nod hello to Mr. Koptev, glancing at Beady on my way out the door. Only when I'm in the hall do I realize he was standing at the right corner of Miss Looping's desk. Hadn't he been on the left when I came in?

CHAPTER 19

'VE BECOME AN EXPERT at avoiding the Karneys. Like eating in the library, it's an acquired skill. No one showers after eight at night, so that's when I shower, and the kitchen is clear by nine thirty, so that's when I get my bedtime drink. It's a skill I won't need much longer, since tomorrow's my birthday, but I cross to the fridge one last time and pour myself a glass of King Karney apple cider. Someone has left their stuff on the table—keys, a wallet, a pack of gum. A camouflage baseball cap that says "Born to Hunt." Dónal's things.

I step closer. The gum is spearmint, like the pack I had in my backpack, only it's half-empty. A bill is sticking far enough out of the wallet to show most of the number 10.

I notice the tear at the corner.

Something about that tear makes me take another step closer. I wiggle the bill out a little further, revealing a second zero. 100.

My fingers tighten around my glass of cider. I figured

he'd have spent the money by now, or at least divvied it up with his pals, but there it is: a hundred dollars that belong to me. A hundred dollars he doesn't intend to give back.

The truth is, I don't care much about the money. I haven't missed it the way I've missed my birthday card or my old notebook with the swan illustration—things Dónal probably trashed since they're of no use to him. But taking back something is better than taking back nothing, and now I have a chance, maybe the only one I'll ever get.

Before I can change my mind, I put down my cider and pull the bill all the way out of the wallet. I take the gum too for good measure.

It feels nice, reclaiming what's mine.

I fold up the bill and smile. I know it's supposed to be for my college fund, but maybe I could use some of it to buy stuff for my brothers. Candy? Tickets to a movie or an amusement park? Extra-large sticky buns from Patsy's Pastries?

"Mom!"

I reel around. Fin is standing just inside the kitchen doorway, lowering a phone to her side and narrowing her eyes on the money in my hands. But she can't be there. I didn't hear her coming. The floor always groans. Why didn't it groan? Does she have the same knack for sneaking as my mother?

"Mom!" Fin calls again.

"What is it, honey?" Mrs. Karney comes up behind Fin in a dressing gown, with Ben on her hip and Clare and Stewey trailing her. *Now* the floor groans.

Fin points across the kitchen at me. "She just stole that hundred-dollar bill from Dónal's wallet." Her voice oozes with hatred.

It's happening again. It can't be happening again. Words fumble and jumble in my head. *No—it wasn't—I didn't—*

"What?" Mrs. Karney shrieks, handing Ben to Clare and stepping into the kitchen. She takes two steps toward me, rolling up her sleeves. "After I let you stay here. Fed you all those meals. You have some nerve."

My instinct is to drop the money and the gum and run. But running will make me look guilty. And I shouldn't have to run. I have every right to be holding these. They're mine.

"What's going on?" Dónal appears behind the others. Icing on the cake.

"This little crook just took your money." Mrs. Karney glares at me. "I knew we couldn't trust her."

Dónal stares over Mrs. Karney's shoulders at the bill in my hand. There's one crook in this house, and we both know who it is. He could tell everyone right now and clear this whole thing up.

"Yikes." Dónal scratches his head. "That's messed up."

Of course. If he tells them, then he'll have to admit what he did. And he's too much of a coward to do that.

"If she won't leave on her own, the police can deal with her," Mrs. Karney says. "Her mother's negligence is their problem, not mine. Where's my phone?"

"Wait." Conn pushes past his siblings and steps in front of Mrs. Karney. When did he get here? How much has he seen? "Don't you think that's a little drastic, calling the police? Let's just calm down, okay?"

"Don't tell me to calm down." Mrs. Karney flails her arms. "She just tried to take a hundred dollars, and who knows what else she's stolen from us? I want her out of my house. Clare, go get your father. He'll want to know about this."

Clare scurries off with Ben. Conn frowns at the money in my statue fingers and then turns to Dónal. "That's your hundred bucks, bro? Where'd you get it?"

Dónal meets Conn's eyes, blinking once. "Aunt Geraldine. Leftover Christmas money."

Mrs. Karney nods. "Right, she always gives you a little

more since you're the oldest. And that's beside the point."
She's way too eager to believe Dónal's innocence over mine.

"Are you seriously going to just stand there?" Fin
interrupts Conn and Dónal's stare-down. I realize with a
twinge of dread that she's talking to me. "Don't you have
anything to say for yourself?" Her pitch rises. "What's
wrong with you?"

"Fin, chill out," Conn says.

She flashes him a look. "Why are you still sticking up
for her?"

"We don't know for sure what happened. We can't
prove that—"

"Wanna bet?" Fin holds out the phone she's been
clutching, and everyone turns to her. "When I saw Elise
looking at Dónal's wallet, I got this bad feeling, so I grabbed
Mom's phone off the counter. Caught it on video." She taps
the screen, and Conn, Mrs. Karney, Dónal, and Stewey all
watch something I can't see. Then I hear the audio playback
of Fin's voice calling "Mom!" and my stomach churns. The
room spins.

Fin puts the phone on the counter, and I feel dizzy,
distant, like I'm floating near the ceiling, watching this
happen to someone else. "So there's your proof," she says.

Conn blinks and stares at the phone. "I just...don't think she'd do something like this."

"You just *saw* her do it." Fin throws up her hands. "You're unbelievable."

He shakes his head. "There has to be some other explanation."

"Then why don't you let her explain?"

"But she doesn't ta—"

"She *can* talk. We've both heard her. Our first day at school. And at the pastry shop. Her tongue works fine, so drop the act."

Conn's cheeks redden. I've never seen him and Fin fight before.

When I get to be with my brothers, we'll never fight, ever.

"If she somehow wasn't stealing," Fin says, "though clearly she *was*, she'd deny it. She'd have said something by now."

Conn rubs the back of his neck. Everyone in the kitchen has gone quiet. He looks at the tile floor and nods. "You have a point."

Why is he saying that? There's a look on his face—the same look Mel had that last day I sat at her lunch table, when she'd grown tired of defending me.

"Well?" Fin turns back to me. "No one's going to make excuses for you now. Care to explain why you stole from Dónal? And pointed that gun at him?"

"Gun?" Mrs. Karney gasps. "She pointed a gun at my son?" She looks at Dónal. "Is this true?"

Dónal runs a hand over his stubble for effect. "I didn't want to make a big deal out of it..." He's enjoying this, just like he enjoyed stealing my stuff in the woods.

I sway, knowing every word I don't say is working against me, thickening the wall between me and Conn, the one whose trust lasted the longest. This couldn't have been what Granny P had in mind. Maybe a word or two won't matter. Maybe Granny P didn't mean what she said. Maybe I even misheard her. Can I chance it? If I do, will the truth come out right? Nothing ever comes out right. But if I don't try...

"See," Fin says. "She's not even denying it."

Everyone is watching me, waiting, and words keep rising up my throat and then sliding back down. *I didn't...* *It wasn't...* I can feel the bubble pressing in on me, blocking me, choking me. Before I or anyone else can blink, I drop the money and the gum on the counter and fly out the kitchen's side door, shooting through the living room and up the stairs. I run as if the gun just went off at a track meet. In the spare room, I shut the door and take big gulps of air, my heart racing. The bubble's never been that strong before, and I don't know what to think.

All I know is that running away didn't look good. But even if I could have spoken, would it have mattered? If I told the truth, who would they have believed: me, the guest, the stranger, the quiet one? Or Dónal, the loving son and brother? They'd think I was lying, and I'd have broken my promise to Granny P in the process. I shouldn't have tried to risk it all now, when I'm so close to my birthday, so close to the finish line. I've come this far; I've been through the woods and back. I've let my grades slip. I've lost Mel. I've lost Fin. And now Conn. And for what?

Not for nothing. I won't let it be for nothing.

Maybe there's still a way to tell Conn. I stumble over beach and ski gear as I grab my notebook. I scribble words: Dónal's lying. The money and gum are mine. He stole them.

I rip out the page and look at the note. It's barely legible and sounds like a lie even to me. I hear footsteps coming down the hall. Who am I kidding? I have to face it: a note isn't going to help me this time.

I crush the note in my fist and chuck it in the trash bin. I'm wearing pajamas, but there's no time to change. I pull on my sneakers without tying them, stuff some clothes in my school bag, and open the window. It's lucky that I'm on the first floor. I jump, tumbling into a flower bed and the chill of the night air. I consider my options as I run. If it were a lifetime ago, I could go to Mel's house. But a different Mel lives there now. And how can I go home before I've gotten the answers I left for in the first place? Home to boyish echoes and dirty dishes and purplish rings around my mother's eyes?

Twenty minutes later, I find myself huddling on a bench outside Green Pasture, blinking under a security light. I pull my school planner out of my bag and look at the date. April 12th.

Tomorrow is the thirteenth. My birthday.

I breathe in.

Tomorrow.

I breathe out.

Tomorrow, Granny P will bring me my birthday present. I'll get to see my brothers, and everything will be put right.

Tomorrow.

CHAPTER 20

I JERK TO ATTENTION AS a bus screeches in front of the school. I stand and smooth out my hair, hoping no one saw me dozing in my pajamas.

Inside, Green Pasture is so still that my footsteps echo. I'm the early bird. I like the halls this way, without all the students, but maybe I should walk back outside before they start swarming in and anyone knows I'm here. Maybe I should skip school today and forever.

But my ghazal for Miss Looping is due today. Presentations aren't until Monday, and I'll be in the bathroom stall that period if I come to school at all. But the poem itself must be handed in this afternoon, or I'll fail the assignment. I can't afford that.

I go to the bathroom, fish a T-shirt and jeans out of my backpack, and change into them. Then I read in the stall until the first bell rings. After that, I keep my head down. The first three periods consist of ignoring other kids' stares and whispers. And expecting the police to burst in at any moment and arrest me, even though I did nothing wrong. Even though I left the money behind and I'm out of the Karneys' house and I'm just being paranoid. There's no reason they'd call the police now. Is there?

When the lunch bell finally sounds, I head for the track. I won't be able to hog a bathroom stall for the whole lunch hour without people knocking, and I can't go to the library in case Conn's there. Or maybe he'll be avoiding it today too because he thinks I'll be there. Either way, the track is the next best choice. At least there I can get some fresh air.

I set my bag down in the top right corner of the bleachers, the very last row, and make myself comfortable. A lot of people don't sit this high up because they're scared of heights, but it doesn't bother me. The closer to the sky and the farther from school, the better.

A few pages into my book, I notice bright colors approaching, coming up the steps from the bottom of the bleachers.

Why did I think anywhere at Green Pasture might be safe?

"Look who we found."

I'm reading. Unavailable. Otherwise engaged.

"Anyone got a nail clipper?" Sylvia says. "I have a hangnail."

I don't look up, but I can feel the Flock gathering in front of me. This is going to make it hard to read.

"Here's mine." Theresa's voice.

I ought to turn the page and make this reading thing more convincing. But my body is acting like a brick, refusing to move.

Snip. "We heard about what you did." *Snip*. *Snip*. Sylvia stands in the row below me, flicking the pink nail clippings at me one at a time. They bounce off my chest and forehead and land in my book. "Pointing a gun at Fin's brother. And stealing. Fin sent us the video. That's pretty twisted."

My palms start to sweat. Who else has the video gotten around to? Is that why everyone was whispering and staring at me today? I shouldn't have come to school. Who cares about my ghazal? Miss Looping probably won't like it anyway.

"She doesn't even look sorry," Nellie says.

"Her heart must be made of ice." Theresa grunts.

Sylvia hands the nail clipper back to Theresa. "So, why'd you do those things?" She snatches the feather out of my hair and tickles my face with it. She runs it under my chin and down my neck.

I try to grab the feather back.

The Flock laughs in the row behind Sylvia. Fin, Nellie, Theresa... I don't see Mel.

Sylvia tosses the feather aside. I watch the wind carry it away, the only hint of my brothers and Granny P that I had left. "You know, Elise...when you do one of our friends wrong, when you do her family wrong, you do us all wrong. We take it personally."

I stare at my book, at words I can't make sense of.

Fin steps over a seat board and stands next to Sylvia. "It's the quiet ones you have to watch out for," she says, the same way Mrs. Karney did. Maybe she has more in common with her mother than she thinks. "You thought you could threaten and steal from my family? And still keep Conn trailing after you? Well, guess what. You can't." She spits the word *can't*. "Conn wants nothing to do with you. He stays with me. I'm his sister. Best friend. Nothing's bigger than that, not even your pretty eyebrows."

An eyebrow remark. She must have learned that one from Sylvia.

"Got it?" She puts one foot on the seat board between us and rests her elbow on it, leaning forward. Something glints in her other hand at her side. A memory comes to me: Fin at the Karney dinner table on my first night, filing her nails with her Swiss Army knife. She wouldn't... She couldn't...

My body snaps into action—snaps my book shut. I stand up and turn to move toward the aisle, but Fin leaps over the seat board and steps in my way, knocking my book out of my hands. "Where do you think you're going?"

If I could get by, I could run fast. I'm faster than any of them. But now Sylvia, Nellie, and Theresa are moving in, cornering me, ready to snatch and scratch me with their neon claws. I'm outnumbered, just like in the woods with Dónal and his pals.

A bird could fly away.

I look up, finding the sky. I want to be the sun, out of reach up there with the clouds.

"Hello-o-o?" Fin raps her knuckles on my forehead. "Anyone home?" The others laugh.

"Wait."

The Flock turns in unison toward the bottom of the bleachers. Mel's green-lidded eyes meet mine, and for a second I think she's going to come take my hand and lead me away, and we'll go to her house and make one of our "movies." For a second I think she's the person I knew—and I'm the person she knew—before all this.

"I'll talk to her."

"You don't have to, Mel," Fin says. I don't like the way she says *Mel*, as if she's known Mel since she was five. None of these girls have known Mel as long as I have. She has a history with me that none of them, not even Sylvia, can ever have with her.

"I want to." Mel comes up the steps.

Fin nods, and as she moves out of Mel's way, I realize the glint I saw was just a bracelet she's wearing.

Mel stands in front of me, her fists clenching at her sides. "So, is it true?" she says. "Did you really point a gun at Fin's brother? Did you really try to steal from the Karneys? From people who were helping you?" The disgust in her voice makes my insides shrivel. "I don't even know you anymore. If you didn't do it, you'd say so. You'd say something." Mel lowers her voice now, whispering. "Why won't you say *something*? Not even to me?" I catch a hint of pleading in her tone. Desperation. It surprises me. She's giving me one more chance.

Oh, Mel. Pretty Mel, patient Mel…

But she doesn't understand. She's never understood, as much as I've wanted her to. I can't give in now after coming this far, not when I'm so close to getting my brothers back. *I'm sorry, Mel.*

She straightens. I glance up in time to spot a droplet of

water on her cheek before she turns away. I feel one on mine too. Sylvia looks at Mel, and her usual smirk vanishes. Now there's a flicker of something as she glances from Mel to me. I've seen it a few times before, when Mel would stick up for me at lunch, but maybe I never understood what it was.

Remember, she's just jealous, my mother said that afternoon after Patsy's Pastries. A passing comment, but...

No, no one could be jealous of *me*.

"I give up." Mel's voice reverts to a volume the others can hear. "She's a lost cause. Let's go." She moves past Fin and Sylvia and starts walking back down the bleachers, each step she takes sending a pang through my chest.

"No," Sylvia says. "No way. She thinks she can just ignore us? She thinks she's better than us, even after the things she did? Well, I came here to hear her talk, and I'm not leaving till she does." She skirts by Fin and comes toward me, whipping a nail file out of her pocket. "Come on, open up." She prods my lips with the file. "Say *ahhh*."

The Flock laughs, except for Mel, who keeps moving down the bleachers without looking back.

I reach up to bat Sylvia's hand away. She grabs my wrist and twists it behind my back so fast and hard that I almost cry out.

The laughter dies.

"Hey, we made our point." Fin's voice squeaks behind Sylvia. "Let's just get out of here."

"What's wrong with it, huh?" Sylvia hisses, ignoring Fin. "Your tongue... There must be a reason you don't use it. Is it too long? Too fat? Do you need me to file it down?" Her patience has run out. I, on the other hand, know better than anyone about patience. I press my lips together and try to pull my wrist free. She shoves me against the guardrail, the only thing keeping me from falling off the top of the bleachers.

At the impact my lungs shudder, forcing my lips to part. Sylvia raises the nail file toward my mouth, and I can see up close the scratchy, sandpapery surface. My heart thuds as I imagine how it would feel sliding across my tongue—rubbing, scraping, burning... Before she can make contact, I grab her arm with my free hand and try to kick her, but my pinkie toe smacks a seat board. Water streams from the corners of my eyes.

She pushes me against the guardrail again, and it rattles as if it were built fifty years ago—which it probably was. And as I see the shape of Sylvia's file coming toward me again, as I feel the top of the guardrail pressing into my back, a thought courses through me: What if Sylvia destroys my tongue or I fall from these bleachers—smash into pieces—without anyone having heard my voice?

What if no one will ever know what's inside me?

Stop. Leave me alone.

Suddenly saying these words is all that matters. Surely Granny P will understand, if it means saving my life, saving my voice. This is the time to make an exception. The promise put me here in the first place. Granny P put me here. How could she put me here? But there's no time to be mad at her, no energy to waste on anger right now. As Sylvia's file prods my lips again, harder and harder, I will my vocal cords to vibrate and turn the thoughts in my head into sounds. *Stop. Leave me alone.* Four simple words.

But my throat is tightening, resisting. Refusing. As if there's some kind of gulf between my mind and my body. The bubble is thicker than ever. I thought I could trust it. Why can't I break through? Why can't I say something to save my own life?

There's a whirring sound overhead. Wind and flapping wings. Could that be...?

"What the..." The file hesitates against my lips.

I twist and try to push Sylvia out of the way so I can see

the source of the sound, but beyond her blurred face I can only make out watery splotches of gray.

Then a flash of black.

Kraaa.

"Ow!" Sylvia's nail file ricochets off the bleacher seats. Shouts break out among the Flock. Whatever's happening, now's my chance. I draw up my leg and kick. Sylvia yelps and stumbles back onto the seat board behind her. I scramble down the row toward the aisle.

But then Sylvia is grabbing my ankle, pulling it out from under me, and my stomach smacks the hard aluminum floor.

"Out of the way, all of you."

I squint. Someone greenish is pushing through the Flock toward me—Mel. But she's not the one speaking.

"Let me *through*." Miss Looping is right behind her, ushering the girls aside, finding me on the floor. She helps me to my feet. Sylvia stiffens next to me as the color drains from her face, leaving only her makeup and a fresh red scratch on her forehead.

"Yes, I saw you trip her." Miss Looping glares down at Sylvia. "And Mel here told me what you've been doing." I've never heard her use that tone before, not even when students misbehaved in class. Not even when Beady went missing. "All of you to the principal's. Now." She picks up my backpack and book and touches the small of my back, leading me away. Everyone is yelling, and everything is wrong. I've done what Granny P told me to do—I've waited until my birthday; I haven't said a word to anyone—but still nothing makes sense. And something happened back there: I couldn't speak, even when I tried. Have I lost my voice for good? Where are my brothers? I need to go home. They might be waiting for me there. This could all still be worth it in the end.

As I emerge from the Flock's cluster, with Miss Looping guiding me down off the bleachers, I see that a crowd has gathered to watch. It seems like the whole student body is here—or almost the whole student body. There's one face I can't find.

CHAPTER 21

M iss Looping walks me to her classroom and closes the door. I slump into a desk chair in the front row. Instead of going to her own desk, Miss Looping sits in the one next to me.

"What happened out there, Elise?"

I look down at my lap. Then my jeans blur because I'm crying. I wish I weren't, but I am. Miss Looping reaches over and rubs my back. No one's ever rubbed my back before that I can remember. After a minute she stands, and I wonder if she's given up on me now too.

Then she sets some blank paper and a pen in front of me and tells me to write. I don't know what she means, and she doesn't explain. She just goes to her desk and shuffles through a stack of papers.

I pick up the pen. I'm not sure if the words that come make sense—the unsleep makes it hard to tell—but I write down everything: Mel's seventh birthday party, the shed, the late-night encounter with my mother, the stealing in the woods, the cottage, my brothers, Granny P, the misunderstandings. I guess you can call it a letter, though I don't address it to anyone. I write fast. My wrist hurts from where Sylvia twisted it, and my fingers ache, but the breeze from the window feels nice, so I keep writing.

I don't know how much time has passed. When I finally finish the letter—five pages front and back—I look up. Miss Looping is still at her desk, grading papers. Beady's spot is empty. I was so engrossed in my letter that I hadn't noticed.

Miss Looping sees where I'm looking and sighs. "Yes, he's gone again. Oh well." She shrugs. "Guess he was needed elsewhere." She lowers her eyes back to her papers. The corner of her mouth twitches once.

I find myself forgetting Beady and everything else for a minute and wondering if Miss Looping and her sister looked alike. Did they share secrets? Have a sister language? Did Miss Looping see it coming—the suicide?

I get up and hand her my letter with a note on top. Sorry about your sister.

She reads it and smiles. "Oh. Thanks. It took time, but I'm okay now. You could say I had some help."

I tilt my head inquisitively, and she tucks a curl behind

her ear. "Sometimes when we feel lost, the universe sends a little help. Something or someone to guide us on our path." She chuckles, her eyes gleaming. "And that can come in the most unexpected form."

I try to smile along like I know what she's talking about, because this is how Miss Looping is sometimes—a little, well, loopy. But that's also why I like her.

"This isn't for me, by the way." She sets my note aside but hands my letter back to me without looking at it. "Hang on to it. I don't need to know what happened, but other people will."

I take the letter back to my desk and slip it in a folder in my backpack. I pause at a piece of paper in the folder's left pocket: my ghazal. I almost forgot to hand it in.

I'm a few minutes early to my meeting with Ms. Standish. Her office door is shut, but leaning close I can hear my mother already inside.

"Yes...she talks at home. Well, she hasn't spoken to me lately, but...usually...when she's home...she talks. I mean, I'll ask if she had a good day at school, and she'll say yes. I'll ask what she wants for dinner, and she'll tell me. We never have elaborate conversations, but…" A pause. "You're telling me that all this time, she hasn't been talking at school?"

I press my ear to the door. I've never heard her talk to other people about me. Is she only pretending to be concerned so that she sounds like a "normal" mother in front of Ms. Standish?

"Yes, well, that's what I'd like to discuss. I wasn't fully aware of the problem until the incident at the track today. I knew Elise was quiet, but then I started talking to some of her classmates. They said she hasn't spoken here at all for a week."

"At all?"

"And in the months before that, she averaged a few words a day. Only when spoken to. Now, I understand she was homeschooled before she came here…"

"So?"

"Well, some would say home learners miss out on proper social development, and—"

"Wait a minute." I hear my mother shifting in her chair. "That's a stereotype."

"I know. I was going to say, I don't think that's what's going on here. I know other ex-homeschoolers who have no trouble talking."

I think of Fin and Conn.

Papers shuffle. "Read this when you have a chance."

"'Selective mutism'?" My mother's voice wobbles. "I've never heard of it."

"It's an anxiety condition—usually first noticed when a kid starts school outside the home. That's preschool in many cases. In Elise's case, eighth grade. It sounds like she had low-profile selective mutism for a while, but then it got worse."

I gape at the door. Is she *diagnosing* me? Who does she think she is?

"And if she hasn't been talking to anyone lately, including you, she might even have progressive mutism."

"Progressive?"

"Meaning she started out not talking in certain situations, but now it's progressed to all situations. Bear in mind, I'm a counselor, not a clinical psychologist, so you'd want an expert's opinion. I recommend Dr. Rosetti…"

Anger rattles my bones. What right does Ms. Standish have to analyze me like I'm the subject of a scientific study? I grab the door handle and storm into the office. Ms. Standish and my mother look up. It's the first time I've seen my mother since I hid behind the bush the other day. The new wrinkles on her forehead couldn't be for me. She has never worried over me. Maybe over my brothers, but not me.

"Elise…right on time." Ms. Standish smiles. "Have a seat."

I sit in one of the chairs against the wall opposite my mother.

My mother's eyes fill with watery stuff. Where have these emotions been? The only other time I've ever seen her cry was that moment in the driveway, when she didn't know I could see.

"Elise..." Ms. Standish leans her elbows on her desk and folds her hands. "Is there any way you can explain to your mother and me what happened today? Why you didn't say anything or call for help?"

They both watch me as if waiting for my body to break out in mime or sign language or interpretive dance. I look down at my hands.

That's when I realize why Miss Looping told me to write the letter.

I reach into my backpack and take out the pages, giving them to Ms. Standish. She raises an eyebrow and begins to read, sipping her coffee. After she finishes the first page, she passes it to my mother. Their eyes dart across my words, and I think they forget I'm here. While I wait, I stare at the pamphlet on the chair next to my mother. On the cover, a black-and-white photograph shows a girl sitting in the middle of a classroom, her mouth a line, while the kids around her smile and raise their hands. White letters are printed over the picture: *Selective Mutism*. The girl looks young for someone so solemn. Is that what I look like to other people?

The papers rustle. Ms. Standish hands the last page to my mother and drains her coffee, glancing up at me curiously.

My mother keeps looking from the papers to me to Ms. Standish, her eyes wide.

"Can you judge how much of this is true?" Ms. Standish asks her.

My mother shakes her head. "This... I don't even understand this."

"Do her brothers know about this...account of hers?"

I study my uneven nails, waiting for my mother's answer. She doesn't say anything. I glance up, and she's looking straight at me. "She doesn't have any brothers."

I can't believe her. Here I am, giving away my letter, trying to tell the truth, and she's lying to my face?

"So these two boys... You never had them?" Ms. Standish asks.

"I never said never."

Ms. Standish frowns. "Sorry?"

"I did have them."

"But what—"

"They passed away." My mother's hands tremble as she sets down my letter on the seat next to her. "When she was a baby. They were in a car accident."

I sit up in my chair. Passed away? Why is she saying that?

"Oh." Ms. Standish puts a hand on her chest. "Oh, I'm so sorry. I had no idea." She holds out a tissue box.

My mother takes a tissue and dabs her eyes. "That's why she couldn't have seen them. It's just not possible."

Lies, I want to shout. *Don't let her fool you. Lying is her specialty.*

Ms. Standish taps her chin and looks over at my letter on the chair. "Well, there *is* the possibility..." She hesitates. "You'll see in the pamphlet I gave you that selective mutism often coexists with other types of anxiety. Does Elise seem to worry a lot? Any trouble sleeping?" She doesn't turn her head, but her eyes flit in my direction. "Sleep deprivation can cause hallucinations."

Cold air prickles my neck. Is that an accusation?

I spring to my feet. I refuse to listen to any more of this.

My mother squints at me through puffy eyes. "Are you okay?"

She's suddenly so interested in my well-being. I hurry past her and Ms. Standish, snatching my letter off the chair.

Both of their jaws drop, but they don't have time to object because I'm out the door.

I run all the way home. I think I beat my personal record for the mile. Coach Ewing would be proud.

I burst through the front door and bound through the house, looking in every room and out the windows into the yard. No one is here waiting for me. No Granny P. No boys with eyebrows that almost meet in the middle.

In the kitchen, a few dishes sit in the sink, though not as many as last time. I notice another appointment card for Hillview Counseling & Psychotherapy on the table. And the knitted scarf, still not finished but longer than before. Next to it lies a folder with a sticky note on it and words in my mother's hand: *For Elise*. I open the folder. A few newspaper clippings sit inside. I spread them out, my vision moving in and out of focus across the headlines.

Father dead, sons in critical condition after single-car crash

Young crash victim brain-dead, older brother still fighting

Tragic update to Barmazian brothers' story

I snatch up the last one. The paper shakes because my fingers shake.

BOSTON—Pregnant math professor Moira Barmazian was teaching a class on April 13 when her water broke—a week earlier than expected. A colleague drove her to the hospital and phoned her husband, Greg Barmazian, who was at home with their two sons.

Approximately fifteen minutes later, drivers down the road from the hospital saw Mr. Barmazian's car crash into a guardrail, flip, and roll down an embankment before striking a tree.

Mr. Barmazian was pronounced dead at the scene, while three-year-old Eustace Barmazian and five-year-old Emerson Barmazian were rushed to the hospital where their mother was in labor. It appeared that Mr. Barmazian had not been wearing a seat belt, and his sons had not been properly secured in their car seats.

Doctors later told Mrs. Barmazian that Emerson was drifting in and out of consciousness and might pull through with long-term health complications. Eustace,

however, was on life support and showed no brain
activity or hope of recovery.

I pause, trying to calm my heartbeat. Trying to clear my
head. Barmazian? I don't know that last name. But the first
names match up. My mother's, my brothers'...and the date
of the accident.

I force myself to keep reading.

Yesterday evening, following weeks of silence, the
family finally updated the press. Liesl Pileski, the boys'
grandmother, was in tears as she relayed a message
from their mother, revealing that Mrs. Barmazian had
given doctors permission to switch off Eustace's life
support a week after the accident.

Just three days later, Emerson had suffered bleeding
in his brain and had been put into a medically induced
coma for emergency brain surgery. Once taken off full
sedation, he had remained comatose.

"It's like he followed his brother," said Pileski. "Like
he couldn't be without him." Yesterday morning, Mrs.
Barmazian granted permission to withdraw Emerson's
life support.

CHAPTER 22

I PUSH AWAY THE CLIPPING. My chest heaves.

No—this is wrong. All wrong. I saw them. I heard them. At the cottage in the woods. They were both there, Eustace and Emerson, safe and sound.

I clamp my eyes shut so I can go back.

But when I try to picture the clearing, the cottage, my brothers...I can't see the details. I can't tell Emerson from Eustace. I can't see their faces. I can't see Granny P either. I can't see any of it. It's all a blur, a windshield under broken wipers in the rain. *Sleep deprivation can cause hallucinations...*

There are colors, lots of colors, tumbling together and then apart. The awake and the unsleep, crashing together and then apart.

Was there ever a cottage in the woods? Was there ever music? Two boys and an old woman?

Is Ms. Standish right?

I leave the clippings scattered on the table and stumble out the back door to the shed. Inside, I find the teddy bear in one of the boxes and straighten his bow tie. Smooth out his fur. I wrap my arms around him and curl up on the shed floor like I'm five instead of thirteen.

When I wake up, a blanket covers me. I sit up to find my mother sitting cross-legged near a box behind me, looking at a toy boat in her hand.

"The plan was to give it to you myself," she says. "The folder."

She turns the boat this way and that, studying it from different angles. She still can't look at me.

"But I guess you know now…how it ended." She takes a long breath. "And I hope you don't think I blamed you."

The newspaper clippings flash before my eyes. Doesn't she realize it's a little too late for that? If it weren't for me— if I hadn't come early—my brothers and my father would be here. I'd know them. We'd be an actual family, and my mother wouldn't be so…

I turn away, hiding my face in the crook of my arm. I can't let her see my tears.

"Listen. Do you know why your father crashed that car?" She pauses. "It wasn't because of you."

I shake my head and keep my face in my arm. The newspaper clippings made it clear: He was driving to the hospital. I might not have caused the crash, but he and my brothers wouldn't have been in the car at that moment if it weren't for me.

"One thing we kept from the press..." My mother sighs. "Well, there's no nice way to say it. They found alcohol in your father's system."

I lift my face and turn to stare at her. She told me a drunk driver had killed him. She never said *he* was that driver.

"I know." She presses on. "I should have told you. I should have told you lots of things."

I wipe my eyes and watch her tuck the toy boat inside a box. "I had this idea that I could separate you from what happened. I mean, that's why I gave you my maiden name. That's why I moved us a few towns away and homeschooled you for so long. So you wouldn't have to live in the shadow of a tragedy. But I handled it all wrong." She closes the flaps on the box of toys. "And I shouldn't have hung on to their stuff like this. It never helped, the way I'd come out here some nights just to breathe in their scent."

I think of the two nights I spotted her leaving the shed.

"Maybe tomorrow, if you're free, you can help me bring some of these toys to the charity shop."

I look around at the boxes. It will be a good thing. The toys will find new homes, and children will play with them again, bring them back to life. But my mother said *some*, not *all*, so I tuck the teddy bear under the blanket for safekeeping.

My mother reaches into a box without an *Emerson* or *Eustace* label and pulls out an old photo album. She opens it and scoots toward me, holding it out so I can see. I look on as she flips through baby pictures of my brothers. Sometimes my mother is in them, smiling at the boys, and sometimes a man with a moustache is there too. In one photograph, Emerson is sitting on my father's shoulders while my father smiles at the camera, a beer can in hand. In the background, my mother is watching, frowning. But in another picture, my father is on a couch with my brothers, one on each of his knees, reading a Dr. Seuss book to them. I can tell he loved my brothers. And he would have loved me.

Still, it's funny: I didn't know about my brothers or Granny P until this month, and yet they feel more real to me than my father, who's been a vague figure floating at the back of my mind all my life. And he only grows vaguer now, maybe because I can't understand why he, or anyone, would do something that endangered those he loved. Maybe someday I will, but right now it seems impossible.

We come to a picture of an older woman with my brothers. "That's my mom." My mother taps the woman with her finger.

I squint at the photograph. The old woman's face is out of focus, like the face of the old woman in the woods.

"Some people criticized my decision," my mother says. "Kept saying miracles could happen. But your granny understood. I don't suppose you remember her? She died when you were five."

My stomach sinks. She's dead?

On some level I must have known.

"I should have brought you to see her more often. But I had trouble leaving the house, facing people, back then. That's how I lost friends, lost my job, stopped teaching for a while. Could only manage online classes after that." She keeps her eyes on the photograph. "Right before she died, she kept insisting I tell you everything. I promised her I would when you turned thirteen. I figured you'd be old enough to understand then. And I could put it off a while. Then last weekend you found their stuff in here, and I..." She shakes her head.

"I still couldn't face telling you. Silence was easier. And I realize now what sort of harm that might have done."

She takes something out of her pocket—the Selective Mutism pamphlet—and looks at the girl on the cover. "You must have been frustrated with your own silence. Not knowing how to explain it. I can see how appealing it must have been to think your silence could bring home your brothers." My mother half smiles. "Believe me, I prefer your version." She folds and unfolds the pamphlet, eventually setting it aside. "It's still hard. I still question my decision every day. But I couldn't keep either of them here like that. They weren't *there* anymore. I just..." Her voice trails off, and she presses her lips together.

So that's what she meant. *No one understood why I couldn't keep them here.*

She slides a hand over her graying hair, and it shows—what she's been through. During all the years I mistook for indifference, even resentment, she's been suffering.

And now that the right colors have come into focus, I understand that I've been suffering too. No wonder my mother and I couldn't be there for each other. We couldn't even be there for ourselves.

Next in the photo album we come to a picture of a girl no

older than three, holding a toy telephone to her cheek, her mouth open. My mother smiles. "You were little miss chatterbox."

I stare at the picture. Can that really be me? What happened to her?

My mother takes a deep breath. "I know I haven't been mom of the year. Or the decade. But I need you to know none of it was your fault." She looks me in the eye now. "You know that, right?"

I try not to look away like I normally would. Her eyes are hazel like mine.

She leads me back inside to the kitchen, where she opens the fridge and takes out a cake with shimmery gold icing that says *Happy 13th Birthday, Elise*, kind of like the cakes I've seen at Patsy's Pastries, only nicer. Homemade.

"Thirteen on the thirteenth. Your golden birthday." She gets out two plates and two forks. "Hungry?"

I nod.

"Me too."

As we dig in, I see the curtains flutter once at the open window behind my mother—probably just a breeze. We clean our plates and lick the frosting off our forks. It's a start.

CHAPTER 23

T HE ENTIRE SCHOOL IS reading my letter.

This morning, I gave a note to the librarian—Ms. Defino, as I finally learned she's called—asking for a favor. Now all five double-sided pages of my letter are in the library, in a binder with a bar code and everything, just like a library book. Anyone who wants to know the truth can know.

Sylvia, Fin, Nellie, and Theresa have been suspended, but I heard that photocopies of the letter have gotten around to them. I wonder if Mel has read it yet. I suspect she has, because I found a belated birthday card from her in my locker, small enough to fit through the vent. *We should get milk shakes sometime*, she wrote in the card. I know she and I can never go back to the way it used to be on her front steps. But we can go forward. Even if we don't end up best friends again, we don't need to be enemies. I think I'll go for that milk shake.

I decide to wait until the school day is over before I return to the library. It's been unusually crowded all day. When I get there, Bernard Billows is walking out, folding up a copy of the *Green Pasture Gazette*. He waves and hands me the newspaper. "Congrats, Elise," he says. "Way to go." I'm not sure what he means, but I smile and slip the newspaper into my sweatshirt's front pocket. As he moves past me, I catch a whiff of spoiled milk and think, *Someday that kid's going to be president or a rock star or something and surprise us all.*

I enter the library and stop short. Someone's reading my letter, his back facing me.

When he turns around, he sees me and walks up to me. He stands there for a minute. Then he says, "Want to go see that documentary? It's still playing."

I look across the room at my letter. He isn't going to say anything about it? He isn't going to ask questions?

My eyes fall on a sign on the wall: QUIET IN THE LIBRARY. And I realize that Conn has never asked me for an explanation. Just like he's never called me that word. *Quiet.* Not once.

After the documentary, *Taking Wing*—seventy minutes about the physics of bird wings, how they work—we go for a stroll through the orchard.

"You should've seen my mom's face when she heard you're a Barmazian," Conn says. "She and my dad remember hearing that story on the news."

He tells me about the phone call his family got from Ms. Standish during dinner Friday. I wish I'd been there to hear Ms. Standish read them my letter after asking to be put on speakerphone. To see Mrs. Karney's mouth hang open and Mr. Karney's brow furrow. To see Fin run into Dónal's room, finding a backpack in his closet with my name on the tag, and my old notebook and my birthday card smushed at the bottom. To see Dónal's face turn apple red and hear him stumble on words as everyone turned to him demanding the truth. To see him squirm, sweat, admit to everything, all while trying to blame it on his hunting pals. To see Conn's jaws tighten while he listened to it all.

"My dad and I dropped your stuff off Saturday," he says. "Did your mom give it to you?"

I nod. I stayed in my room while he and Mr. Karney were talking to my mother at the door—I wasn't ready to see any Karneys yet—but I checked my backpack later, and everything was in it, including my college money. And my old tallies, but I tossed those in the recycling bin.

"Dónal's grounded," Conn says as we sit down under

an apple tree. "Mark and Dakota are in hot water too. My mom called their parents, and guess what? All three of them got their hunting licenses revoked. Turns out Dónal lied to my parents and told them Mark's eighteen. Licensed minors have to be accompanied by a licensed adult while hunting, but they're all still seventeen. *How* sad."

I have to admit that's pretty satisfying news.

"Then there's Fin. She isn't ready to talk to you yet, but she'll be knocking on your door soon. She just needs time. She knows when she's wrong, and she's embarrassed. Plus...I think she's kind of jealous of you. She's used to being my main girl."

He turns his crooked smile on me, and I feel my cheeks catching fire, the way they did when Sylvia asked if he was my boyfriend. I try to focus on the grass blades in front of me, but my frame of vision keeps sliding to my periphery, where Conn is watching me. My stomach floats to my chest. *Don't look. Don't look.* Are his cheeks on fire too? Why do I care?

Maybe I only feel this way because he was the first boy to ask me to a movie—or at least a documentary. The first boy to sit with me at the library. The first boy to pay me any notice really. I guess those firsts can get to a person's head. At least he wasn't there at the bleachers to see what happened.

He might have tried to rescue me, and I wouldn't want that getting to my head too. Because the truth is, it's best that we're just friends for now. My attention has to be on school. And on getting better. On going to my first appointment with Dr. Rosetti next week, even though the thought scares the heck out of me.

I'm tempted to go back into the woods right now, retracing my steps toward the cottage to see what's really there. If anything's there at all. But I decide not to. I want to keep that world like a memory. I still feel that world existing in a cottage deep in the woods, where my brothers are safe— where they'll always be safe.

A flash of black breaks my rumination.

"What's wrong?" Conn follows my gaze to the branch of a tree on our right. "Oh, hey, Mister Crow." He frowns. "No, wait." He whips his binoculars up to the bridge of his nose. "My mistake. That's a raven."

Goose bumps travel up my arms.

"Lots of people confuse them with crows, but up close you can spot the differences. Ravens are twice the size. With a stronger bill, longer wings. Shaggy feathers at the throat, see?" He passes me the binoculars. I take a deep breath and look through them, finding the raven. He stares back in a perfect imitation of Beady. What is it about that stare that has always bothered me?

"And they're not as social as crows. You usually see them alone. Sometimes in pairs or small groups, but usually alone."

I keep peering through the lenses. *Not as social…usually alone…* I had it in my head that "mute" swans were the birds I could relate to most. But maybe ravens and I have a few things in common.

"Gorgeous creatures, aren't they? A little foreboding, sure. They're scavengers, so they get a bad rap. But they're one of the smartest bird species in the world."

The raven keeps watching me, and I him. The longer I stare, the more I see. For some reason, that moment in the woods comes back to me, that horrible moment when Dónal's buddies had me pinned. And that moment on the bleachers, when I thought Sylvia was going to file my tongue off. There had been wings beating. A bird's *kraaa…*

"Is it me, or is he looking right at you?" Conn laughs. "Seems like he only has eyes for Elise."

The goose bumps spread all over. I think of the silhouette behind my window shade. The *tap-tap-tap* that drew my attention to the shed. The bird that flitted through the woods toward the cottage. The bird that landed on Granny P's shoulder—watching me with the same stare as this guy in the tree. The same stare as Beady on Miss Looping's desk.

Sometimes when we feel lost, the universe sends a little help. Miss Looping's words float on the air. *Something or someone to guide us on our path. And that can come in the most unexpected form.*

Warmth tingles across my scalp. Miss Looping never said what form hers took. But she did say something after Beady first went missing. *I may have bought him on a whim at a thrift shop, but he's been more to me than a decoration.* Now I wonder what she meant. Could it be that she experienced something too...with Beady? After her sister died?

"Look!" Conn leaps to his feet. "There. Might be a chickadee. Can I see those binoculars?"

It takes me a moment to break my stare with the raven and hand over the binoculars.

As the other bird lures Conn away, the raven flies down from the tree and alights on the ground a few feet from me, cocking his head.

Will you stay with me? I gaze at him. *Until I'm better?*

He takes a hop forward. Then another. Looking at me, always looking. And of course I know why that stare has bothered me so much: It seems to see right through me.

Through my silences. My excuses. I close my eyes and tilt my face to the sun. I've been good at making excuses. First it was the tally marks. Then the promise. As much as they consoled me for a while, they can't hold now.

I don't want to be a ghost character anymore.

As I stand up, something falls out of my sweatshirt pocket and onto the ground: the *Green Pasture Gazette*. The raven bounds forward again and gives it a curious peck. I pick it up and flip through the pages, stopping at one in the middle where the corner is turned down. My heart leaps.

> Poetry contest winner:
> When I Speak
> A ghazal by Elise Pileski Barmazian

I breathe in the spring air and fold up the newspaper. I don't need to read the rest because I already know what it says.

EPILOGUE

M Y BACKPACK AND I approach the high school doors. Behind them, ninth grade awaits. A new school year. New classes. New teachers. I can see the track on the far hill, waiting for me to hit the ground running. From the outside, the high school looks like a bigger version of Green Pasture. Inside, though, it's going to be different—even if the walls end up being the same burnt orange. I grip my backpack straps hard. Somewhere past these doors today, I'm going to speak.

In the front lobby, I double-check the homeroom number on my schedule. Then I follow the signs and the people.

The homeroom teacher, Mr. Daley—an extreme animal lover judging by the Animal Planet posters smothering his walls—looks at the roster and tells us that instead of calling roll the boring way, he wants to go around the room and have us each introduce ourselves by saying our name and favorite animal. Some students snicker at the childishness of the activity, but I have other things on my mind.

"Zoe Zhang—um, dolphins, I guess."

"Mario Alvarez—penguins."

"Bridget Flaherty—unicorns."

"Those don't count as... Never mind. Next please?"

Mr. Daley checks off names as the target moves swiftly toward me.

Eleven people away. Ten. Nine.

I sit up in my chair. There's no knowing how my voice will sound when it comes out. There's no knowing *if* it will come out here, as it does in some other places, like home and Dr. Rosetti's office and Mel's house. And if it does come out here, who knows how long it will stay?

People will be watching me, waiting, but that's inevitable. If someone used to have an eating disorder, people who know will always watch how that person eats. If someone used to have a drinking problem, people who know will always watch how that person drinks. And if someone used to have selective mutism, people who know will always watch how that person speaks. *Quiet* feels inked in me like a tattoo. One day I'll be someplace, maybe college, where no one knows I have the tattoo, but for now, if I want to move forward, I'll have to let people look on while I heal. While the tattoo fades beneath my clothes—beneath my feathers.

"Abe Packard—kangaroos. No, rhinos. Maybe lions…"

"Let's go with lions. Next?"

"Marilyn Castino—ferrets."

"Jules Greco—pandas."

Two people away. One.

Something *kraaa*s outside the window.

I breathe in, part my lips, spread my wings.

And fly.

When I Speak

A ghazal by Elise Pileski Barmazian

Words like to crumble and fade when I speak,

clash like a stumbling parade when I speak.

Each little utterance quavers with fear

of the next sound to be made when I speak.

As the words edge past my lips, feel them shake,

knowing a price must be paid when I speak.

Secrets have slipped off my tongue, haunting me;

friends might be lost and betrayed when I speak.

Ears: They will judge me, and even by one

stuttering word they are swayed when I s-s-speak.

When I say nothing, my mind is composed.

But all ideas become frayed. When. I. Speak.

I hear the world, but they can't hear me

waging an inner crusade when I speak!

Let them all dub me the quiet one now.

Someday they'll hear words cascade when I speak.

AUTHOR'S NOTE

While *After Zero* is a work of fiction loosely inspired by the Brothers Grimm tale "The Twelve Brothers," the moments in which Elise experiences anxiety about speaking are inspired by my past adolescent experience with low-profile selective mutism. As with many other kids and teens around the world, my struggle with this anxiety condition went unrecognized and undiagnosed. This is understandable, considering the lack of public awareness and knowledge of not only selective mutism in general, but also the differences between low-profile and high-profile selective mutism. Each person's experience is nuanced and unique, but generally, individuals with selective mutism speak freely in at least one situation (such as home). However, in certain other situations (such as school), those with a high-profile pattern do not speak at all, and those with a low-profile pattern may manage to speak minimally when absolutely necessary but don't initiate contact or make requests. Both experience high anxiety levels in these situations, but low-profile selective mutism is more likely to be overlooked or dismissed as shyness because it is less obvious.

I didn't even encounter the term "selective mutism" until I was in college and had thankfully already overcome the worst of this condition on my own. Fortunately, my selective mutism never got as bad as Elise's does in the second half of *After Zero*, but both high- and low-profile patterns of selective mutism do have the potential to grow worse if unaddressed, even to the rare point where all situations eventually trigger silence (known as progressive mutism). It's important to note that selective mutism should not be confused with traumatic mutism (total mutism that begins suddenly as a symptom of posttraumatic stress), which we see more often in fiction. There's no causal link between trauma and selective mutism, and this anxiety condition can affect anyone, including kids with a loving family like I had.

If you or someone you know can relate to Elise's struggle with anxiety and speaking, you are not alone, and help is available. For more information, check out selectivemutism.org or the following recommended books. And remember, your silence does not define you.

Recommended Resources

The Selective Mutism Resource Manual, 2nd edition,
by Maggie Johnson and Alison Wintgens

Selective Mutism in Our Own Words: Experiences in Childhood and Adulthood by Carl Sutton and Cheryl Forrester

ACKNOWLEDGMENTS

After Zero could not have hatched from a manuscript into a published book without the help and guidance of certain people. I want to thank Becky Bagnell, my wonderful agent at the Lindsay Literary Agency, for seeing promise in my prose and patiently championing my work; Allison Hellegers at Rights People, for finding *After Zero* the perfect home at Sourcebooks; Kate Prosswimmer, my brilliant editor, for "getting" Elise's story and taking it under her wing (final bird pun, I promise) with such care, enthusiasm, and ingenuity; and the whole Sourcebooks Jabberwocky team, for working hard toward a final product with which I couldn't be happier.

Immense thanks also to Queen's University Belfast, including the Seamus Heaney Centre for Poetry and the School of Arts, English and Languages, for the generous funding that allowed me time and space to revise *After Zero*; Dr. Garrett Carr, for his valuable advice and feedback; the MFA program at George Mason University, for the funding that first liberated me so I could pursue creative writing with full force; Erica Little, Lisa Kennedy, Courtney Brkic, Dr. Geralyn Prosswimmer, and everyone else who at some point gave me feedback on drafts or parts of *After Zero*; the Kimmel Harding Nelson Center for the Arts, for my first paid writing residency, during which I worked on an early draft of *After Zero*; Bill Roorbach, Courtney Brkic, and all the teachers, professors, classmates, and friends who have fostered my writing over the years or helped me on my road to publication; and Susan Elizabeth Sweeney, who nurtured my early explorations of "silent sister" tales such as the Grimms' "The Twelve Brothers," which loosely inspired *After Zero*.

Above all, love and gratitude to my family. Dad (who's always there for me and who sparked my love of stories by reading to me when I was wee), Mom (whose unwavering support and encouragement I'd be lost without), Brian (who's a ray of sunshine in my life and the best brother anyone could ask for), and Auntie and Unc (whose excitement about all of my endeavors has meant so much to me)—I don't know where I'd be without you all. And last but positively not least, Rory, thank you for cheering me on, letting me bounce ideas off you, and making me smile every step of the way.

ABOUT THE AUTHOR

Christina Collins grew up in a small town in Massachusetts, devouring fairy tales, looking for secret gardens, and using "wicked" as an adverb. Now she lives across the pond in Northern Ireland, where she is finishing a PhD in creative writing at Queen's University Belfast. She holds an MFA in creative writing from George Mason University and has been a writer-in-residence at the Kimmel Harding Nelson Center for the Arts as well as the Art Commune program in Armenia. *After Zero* is her first novel.